War School

JULIAN MANIESON

War School

Published by The Conrad Press in the United Kingdom 2018

Tel: +44(0)1227 472 874
www.theconradpress.com
info@theconradpress.com

ISBN 978-1-911546-22-1

Typesetting and Cover Design by:
Charlotte Mouncey, www.bookstyle.co.uk

The Conrad Press logo was designed by Maria Priestley.

Printed and bound in Great Britain by Clays Ltd, Elcograf S.p.A.

For Mrs Roberts
You were right!

PART ONE:

A School for Warriors

1
Trouble at School

'Well, does anyone have an answer?'

Hugo shot his right hand up in the air.

The teacher, Miss Weiss, caught Hugo's eye and smiled. She looked around the class for another suggestion before nodding at him.

'Seventy-five degrees, Miss,' said Hugo.

Miss Weiss's smile broadened.

'Thank you, Hugo.' She wrote the answer on the blackboard.

Hugo Safin was average at maths, nothing special, but it was Friday afternoon and he was the only one in his class who could be bothered to answer any questions.

As he spoke, a few of the other pupils glared at him. Hugo was aware of the glares but didn't react; he'd become used to them by now.

'Miss Weiss!' The voice belonged to a large thuggish boy called Klaus Holzmann. He was the son of the town's Gestapo officer.

'Yes, Klaus, what is it?' Miss Weiss replied, 'and there's no need to shout. This is a classroom, not a Nuremburg rally!'

'Oh yes Miss, there's no doubt about that,' Klaus said, pausing for effect, 'because if it was a Nuremburg rally...' Klaus pointed the grimy nail of his right forefinger at Hugo, 'this piece of Russian scum wouldn't be allowed here!'

'Shut up, Klaus!' Hugo said.

'That's quite enough,' Miss Weiss told them. 'Klaus, apologise to Hugo. Hugo's mother was born in Russia, yes, but his father was a loyal German!'

'I don't believe it!' shouted Klaus. He clenched his fists and strode out of the classroom.

'Come back, Klaus!' Miss Weiss called, but it was of no use.

Their mother always insisted that Hugo and Lottie walk home from school together, for safety; and so Hugo found himself waiting just inside the front gates for almost twenty minutes until his sister emerged from the building.

'Where've you been?' Hugo asked her, relieved that she'd finally arrived.

'I was talking to that woman from the art school again,' Lottie said.

'The one visiting from Berlin?' Hugo asked.

Lottie nodded. 'They're offering a full scholarship now, as well as food and accommodation.'

Lottie had her brother's blonde hair, but she had bright green eyes instead of brown. At fourteen, she was a year younger than Hugo, and yet for the most part she was louder and more confident.

'What did you say?' Hugo asked.

Lottie's eyes narrowed. 'What do you think? Mother's made it pretty clear every time I've mentioned it. "You aren't going anywhere unless it's together."'

'Well, it's for the best,' Hugo said.

'For you maybe,' Lottie muttered icily.

'We should probably go home,' Hugo said, 'We're late as it is.'

'Whatever,' Lottie glared at her brother.

Hugo went through the gates first, with his sister in tow.

As soon as they were both clear, Hugo felt something move quickly beside him and a large hand grabbed his right arm and pulled him aside.

'Come with me,' Klaus said darkly. He kept a fist of Hugo's shirt in his hand and led him round the side of the school building.

'What are you doing?' Lottie shouted out.

The change Lottie provoked in Klaus was almost comical. The menacing look evaporated and he unclenched his fists, releasing Hugo. His left hand, which had been gripping Hugo's shirt moments before, flew up to his own dark hair and tousled it in an attempt to smarten himself. Finding himself suddenly released, Hugo tried to edge away, but found his shirt caught in Klaus's grip again. He was going nowhere.

'I asked you what you were doing!' Lottie said.

Klaus opened his mouth to say something, but Hugo cut across him.

'Lottie, could you tell him to get lost?' He realised how pathetic it was to ask his little sister to do it for him, but he knew Klaus had a soft spot for her, and he was in no position not to exploit it.

'Leave us alone, Klaus, please,' Lottie said to Klaus sternly. She walked off alone, so annoyed with Hugo's not supporting her about the scholarship, that she flouted their mother's rule about staying together.

'Wait!' Klaus shouted at her back. Lottie swivelled to face him. 'I was wondering...' Klaus asked haltingly, 'if you aren't doing anything on...'

'I'm not, but the answer is no. You're about to attack my brother and are asking me out at the same time? Are you insane?'

'I…' Klaus began.

'Forget it!' Lottie said finally, 'don't you dare do anything to Hugo!' she added ferociously. Klaus, far being from the imposing young man he had been minutes before, seemed to shrink under her gaze.

Confident in Klaus' deference, Lottie swivelled on her heels and began to make her way home.

Klaus sighed as Lottie continued to walk away. 'It was worth a try,' he said quietly to himself. He waited until Lottie had turned the corner and couldn't see them any more before turning his attention back to Hugo.

'Just leave me alone, Klaus,' Hugo said. He'd lost his only real defence in his sister, and could see that Klaus didn't intend to let him walk away unscathed.

'I don't think that's going to be possible,' Klaus said, with cruel sincerity. Hugo briefly entertained the thought of making a stand, but the maxim 'cowards live longer' came to mind, and he stepped to Klaus's side and attempted to run away.

Klaus had seen this coming, mirrored Hugo's step and thrust his clenched fist into Hugo's gut.

Hugo dropped like a stone, hitting the floor on his chest rather than his hands. As soon as Hugo had picked himself up off the floor, Klaus resumed his offensive, throwing a wild punch towards Hugo's head. It whistled past, but Hugo was sure it would have knocked him out if it had connected.

Hugo backed away some more but Klaus kept up his onslaught, all the while shouting abuse at Hugo.

Then, suddenly, Hugo saw a chance to kick at Klaus's legs and took it, and through a blind bit of luck, Klaus tripped and fell over. Hugo didn't feel confident enough to stand over him and gloat, so he stood there, looking a bit gormless, as Klaus got back up.

All Hugo seemed to have succeeded in doing was angering him, but rather than prepare to attack again, Klaus's hand slipped down into his back pocket and came out with a knife.

A chill went over Hugo. He had seen Klaus gut and slice all manner of things with that knife at Hitler Youth camps; it was like an extension of his arm. He and Lottie had only joined the Hitler Youth because if you didn't, the Nazi authorities started to ask questions. Klaus flicked the knife open with vindictive pleasure; and while Hugo didn't think Klaus would go as far as murder, he was certainly looking to do more than just scare him.

Klaus swung out with the blade, and Hugo instinctively grabbed his wrist and tried to wrestle the knife out of his hand.

They both pushed as hard as they could, and a sudden and unexpected lull in force from Klaus's arm caused the knife to lurch back towards the larger boy. Klaus moved his head away, but the blade cut through his shirt and nicked his skin.

'You bastard! You've stabbed me!' Klaus whimpered. Truth be told, it was hardly a scratch, but it didn't take a genius to realise that Klaus would milk it for all it was worth. 'I'm going straight home to tell my father!' Klaus shouted, quickly seeing an opportunity to turn defeat into victory. 'At the very least you'll be arrested for assault.' Klaus spat at Hugo's feet and ran off.

Hugo knew that the last thing his family needed was for Klaus's father, Mr Holzmann, to come knocking, but it seemed inevitable; Hugo lived in Cranz, a suburb of Hamburg and a couple of miles away, whereas Klaus's house was barely a five-minute walk away from the school.

Knowing he had already wasted too much time, Hugo hurried away from the school and towards his house, expecting to see Lottie, who'd gone ahead, but there was no sign of her. He only stopped to clamber through a wooden fence that marked the boundary of a farmer's fields.

Hugo reached the other side of the field without incident, and climbed through the fence to get out. His journey home usually took the best part of half an hour, but the adrenaline coursing through his veins made it feel like ten minutes. He turned the corner of his road with a feeling resembling pride; perhaps he'd beaten Holzmann to his house.

A black car already stood in the drive.

The car was empty: Holzmann must already be at the front door. Moving towards his house, listening for voices, he heard snippets of conversation.

'... I don't believe it,' said Hugo's mother. She stood outside the open door, with a triumphant Holzmann in front of her.

'Mrs Safin, my son came home with a deep wound in his shoulder and he said your son gave it to him,' Holzmann said.

Anna Safin's expression hardened. She stared into Holzmann's eyes.

'Let's not pretend that's why you're here. This is the third time you've come here with a trumped-up charge and tried to get me down to the station for questioning,' Anna said. 'If you keep harassing my family with false accusations, I'll have to go to the authorities.'

'This is not a false accusation, Mrs Safin. Klaus has a nasty wound to prove it. And you'll find I am the authority around here.'

'Then I'll go to your superiors,' Anna said calmly. Holzmann's mood changed immediately.

'Don't you dare talk to me like that!' Holzmann spat. In a fit of rage, he grabbed hold of Anna's hair and pulled her head down. 'Listen, you cow! You'd better start telling me how you Russian bastards have avoided capture for so long, or the only thing my superiors will hear is how you fell underneath my car!'

Hugo ran towards his mother and Holzmann.

'Let go of my mother, you coward!' he yelled at the top of his voice, running towards the two of them. To do what, he didn't know. Holzmann turned to face Hugo, dragging his mother with him onto the porch.

'What will you do if I don't, you little rat?' he sneered. Something about his venomous tone stopped Hugo in his tracks. At best he couldn't see how he could help his mother against a grown man.

'We'll call the police and tell them you're attacking our mother!' Lottie shouted from the doorway. Hugo hadn't noticed his sister come out of the house. She was glaring at Holzmann.

It took Holzmann a whole ten seconds to realise he couldn't salvage the situation. He just stared at them all. Then he yelled at Anna. 'You can't hide forever, you Russian bitch! One day - one day soon - the Gestapo will arrest you and your two brats!' Letting go of her hair, and muttering about calling the police, Holzmann stormed away, got into his car and drove off, narrowly missing Hugo on the way out of the drive.

Hugo and Lottie ran to their mother's side. She was leaning against the pebbledash wall, shaking. The two of them hadn't seen her like this for years. Her eyes were full of tears, and her long blonde hair, usually so straight and shiny, was messy and matted.

'This is the final straw,' she said weakly. 'It's not safe for you here anymore.'

Lottie and Hugo looked at each other, thinking the same thing.

'I'd love to find a way to take you to Russia out of sight of the soldiers, but I can't anymore, what with the war.'

Anna didn't notice the relieved expressions on her children's faces, for she was deep in thought. Hugo and Lottie certainly didn't want to go to Russia.

'I've been toying with an idea for quite some time now. It's time to put it into action.' Anna stood up away from the wall and dusted herself off, 'Lottie, I want you to bring one of your paintings down: that one of the poppy-field will do. Hugo, I want your school reports. Now, please!' she said sharply.

By the time Anna had sat down in the living room, Lottie arrived with a canvas that bore a watercolour of a house amidst rolling hills, and Hugo with a large stack of yellow sheets.

'That's not the one of the poppy-field,' Anna said. Lottie shook her head.

'I thought this one's much better. What do you think?' Lottie asked, holding the canvas up for her mother's inspection. As her mother, Anna had become used to the masterpieces that her daughter had been producing since she was old enough to hold a brush, and so this painting, that would get her into any art school in the country, was set on the table beside a potted plant.

'It's lovely, Lottie,' Anna said. 'When did you do it?'

'I started it last night and I finished this morning before school,' Lottie said, turning to leave the living room. 'I have homework to do, so I'll be upstairs.'

'Supper is at six, darling,' Anna said to her daughter as she left. 'I'll be there,' Lottie said humourlessly, the thought of several straight hours of homework was already dampening her spirits.

'I don't have any homework myself,' Hugo said, placing his reports on the table next to Lottie's painting. 'I was going to go to the park before dinner.'

'Do I have to remind you that you were in a fight this afternoon?' Anna said, suddenly stern, 'and however much it was an accident, a boy ended up wounded,' Anna added, picking up the reports and sifting through them.

'But Klaus pulled the knife on me!' Hugo said incredulously.

'You ought to have turned the other cheek, Hugo,' Anna said firmly.

'He would have punched it!' Hugo retorted. Raising his voice was never a good idea with his mother but, for once, she didn't even look up.

'You're grounded for a week, starting now,' she said. 'And if you keep arguing, you won't have supper tonight either.'

Hugo turned and left the room, seriously considering slamming the door, but his mother reminded him that if he did, she would ground him for two weeks, not just one.

2

Mr Safin

'Hugo?' the voice was soft and streets quieter than it had been during the day, 'can I come in?'

'Sure,' Hugo said, rolling over in his bed and sitting up. It was his sister at his door, and her eyes were red. She had obviously been crying, and she was twisting a bit of her hair around a finger – always a warning sign.

'Sorry to wake you,' Lottie said meekly.

'Don't worry about it for a second,' Hugo said, 'come and sit down.'

'Thanks,' Lottie said, and she shuffled around the corner of his bed to sit beside him.

'What on earth is wrong, Lottie?' Hugo asked

'I was thinking about dad,' Lottie said. Hugo found himself going suddenly tense at the mention of their father; it usually made him feel how Lottie currently looked. He steeled himself, if he started crying Lottie might lose it completely.

Lottie coughed before she spoke again, interpreting her brother's silence as a nod of the head, 'could you tell me what happened that night? I know you've told me before, but I hardly remember it and sometimes it's like it never happened, and so I feel like he's still alive and…' Hugo pulled his sister in close to him and gave her a hug. He

16

didn't say anything before she had calmed down a little, and then he began.

'A couple of weeks after the Nazis came into power he told our mother that he was going to break into the records office and change the Nazi's files on our family,' Hugo said. 'You see, he knew that the records were stored on punched cards and that the cards were read by special machines called tabulators. Dad also knew how to alter the punched card that stored information about the family so that the card wouldn't show we were Jewish.'

The next part was harder for him to say, but he stuck with it.

'Two days after he'd gone, we got a letter that said that he'd been shot dead by a guard after being caught trespassing.' Lottie winced when Hugo said the words 'shot dead', but she did not allow it to deter her.

'Did he manage it?' Lottie asked, 'to change our records?'

'We don't know,' Hugo said, 'but if he hadn't I think something would have happened to us by now. Do you remember what happened to the Kossels?' Lottie nodded solemnly. The sight of Mr and Mrs Kossel, the only other Jews in Cranz, being dragged from their house, screaming and crying, was something Lottie and Hugo would never forget. Almost as shocking as their fear had been their two-year-old son's lack of it. The little boy had played with the Gestapo officer's nose as he'd carried him out, completely oblivious to what was going on and the danger he was in.

Lottie rested on Hugo's shoulder for a long while, thinking. Hugo didn't have the heart to tell her that he was losing feeling in his arm and so he just left her there, hoping that she'd get up.

A few minutes passed and Hugo began to hear her snore.

The correct, brotherly thing to do would have been to pick her up and carry her to her room, but it was late and Hugo didn't feel up for it. Instead, he edged her off his shoulder and onto a corner of his bed before curling up and trying to get back to sleep.

3

Invitation

'Hugo, Lottie,' Anna said. 'I've got amazing news!'

Hugo and Lottie had only just taken off their school shoes and had gone to sit opposite their mother at the dining table, where their supper was waiting: fish soup, black rye bread, roast chicken with potatoes and a cheese and tomato salad.

'What is it, Mother?' Hugo asked

Anna produced two letters from underneath the table.

'Have either of you heard of War School?' she asked, handing each of them a letter. The letters were cream coloured, had gold piping around the edges and a black swastika centred at the top.

Hugo's letter read as follows:

Hugo Safin, congratulations!

You have been accepted into the most prestigious institution in the Reich, War School. Your orientation is scheduled for 12:00 on Sunday October 12 1941. You have been placed in Hitler house, details of which are in the enclosed brochure.

Best regards,

Adolf von Ribbentrop

Director, War School

'So what is this place, War School?' Lottie asked after she had read her own letter, which placed her in Nuremburg house.

'It's an academy for intelligent and talented German boys and girls, training them for top jobs in the Nazi government and in the military,' Anna replied. 'Of course, girls aren't allowed to fight, but there are many administrative jobs for women in the government and I've heard that, in the future, more women will be given management jobs in the army.'

'Where is War School?' Hugo asked.

'About a hundred kilometres north of here in Kiel, close to the Danish border,' Anna replied.

'Hitler would say that there's no Danish border any more, mother,' said Hugo. 'He'd say that, now Germany has invaded Denmark, it's all part of Germany.'

'Well, my dear, Hitler says a fair few things we don't agree with, doesn't he,' Anna replied.

Lottie picked up the brochure, and read aloud, 'War School has four houses: Hitler house, Nuremburg house, Fatherland house and Victory house. Hitler house is for children with the ability to become generals. Nuremburg house is for artistically gifted children, who will be trained in map-making and invasion strategy. Fatherland house is for maths and science experts and Victory house is for sporty children.'

'Mother, why do you want us to go to this War School place?' Hugo asked. 'Surely we'll be in even more danger there?'

'No, there you'll be safe from people like the Holzmanns,' Anna replied. 'I was actually very, very lucky to get the two of you in.'

'How do you mean?' Lottie asked.

'They called a few days after I sent your applications in last week,' Anna said. 'I didn't mention it to you at the time; it was totally nerve-wracking. They did a lot of research into the family, and found the record of me changing my name, but not, thank God, any record of what your wonderfully brave father seems to have successfully done to save us.'

Hugo and Lottie looked at their mother expectantly, the knowledge that they had been accepted into War School tempering the nervousness inspired by the Nazis probing into their family history.

Anna drew a breath. 'It worked out in our favour, thank goodness. They asked if I was born in Russia and I said yes, then they asked if you both spoke Russian and I told them that you do speak it, but that we speak German here at home. I also said to them that you keep your Russian up by practising it with each other sometimes. It was strange, when I said that, suddenly they seemed really keen to have you at War School.'

'Maybe it's for the war against Russia,' Hugo said. 'Perhaps they want translators.'

'Perhaps,' Anna said, 'I expect the two of you to be practising your Russian from now until you leave for War School, you never know what they will ask of you.'

'Yes, mother,' Hugo and Lottie said, pretty much in unison.

'Good,' Anna said. 'Is there anything else?'

'What will you do with the house to yourself?' Hugo asked.

Anna looked thoughtful. 'I think I will take up the piano again and look around in town for a new piano teacher; the upright's been standing unused for far too long.'

'That sounds like a great thing for you to do, Mother,' Hugo said. He knew that his mother played the piano beautifully, and before he'd been born, she had considered a career as a pianist.

'Are we going to be staying somewhere in Kiel? I mean we can hardly make the journey from here to the school every morning,' Lottie asked

'Yes, of course, it's a boarding school, darling,' Anna replied. 'Every student has their own room.'

'Will we be able to come back at weekends?' Hugo asked.

Anna shook her head. 'I'm afraid not. After all,' she added, 'there is a war on.'

Hugo didn't mind too much about not coming back at weekends, though he knew he'd miss his mother. It wasn't like there were masses of friends he would be leaving behind.

In contrast, Lottie minded a great deal, her frame slumped and she looked upset.

Anna looked at her daughter lovingly. 'I know you'll miss your friends,' she said, before turning to Hugo as well, 'and I'll miss you more than you can know, but your safety is far more important than any of that. Besides, I'm sure you'll make some new friends at War School, There must be some nice people there, even at a school that trains Nazis.'

Lottie and Hugo both nodded, and Anna smiled before moving around the table to hug them.

4

Packing

'How are you doing?'

Anna asked the question as she poked her head around the door of Hugo's room.

As usual, his room looked like a bomb had gone off in it. The clothes alone made it impossible to see the carpet; the bed had books piled high on top; and Hugo himself was standing in the middle of his room, a pair of black underpants in one hand and an old diary in the other.

On a chest of drawers on the far side of the room were more books and a chessboard with wooden pieces all ready for action. Hugo played chess pretty well; Lottie did too, but Hugo was better.

'Fine, thanks,' Hugo said absentmindedly. Anna's eyes swept around the room and she stepped inside, closing the door behind her.

'Well it's tidier than it is usually,' Anna said, 'though that isn't saying much. Do remember that the car's coming to get you and Lottie at ten o'clock tomorrow morning, and you absolutely need to be ready, both of you.'

'Of course, Mother, we will be. Even Lottie can pack in time if she's given a whole day to do it,' Hugo said, throwing both the underwear and the book into a suitcase. 'How long will we be staying at this War School place, anyway?'

Anna took a step into Hugo's room and closed the door behind her.

'That all depends on how the war goes, doesn't it?'

'What do you mean, Mother?' Hugo asked.

'If the end of the war comes, and Germany has won,' Anna said, 'you'll be there until you're adult, then you'll join the Nazi Party.'

Hugo thought for a second. If he did end up a high-ranking Nazi, what would he do? He could hardly sign death warrants, especially if it was just to keep up a cover.

'What if the British win?' Hugo asked.

'I suppose they'd arrest all the Nazis and tear War School down,' Anna said. 'But right now, we are living in a terrible time and must try our best to stay alive.'

'Mother, what about Switzerland?' Hugo asked. 'We could go there and stay with...' he trailed off, avoiding another topic that was rarely brought up: his father or, rather, his father's family.

His grandparents on his father's side had immigrated to Switzerland a few months before the Nazis came into power. They were wealthy, and lived in a huge house on the outskirts of Zurich.

'I really wish we could go there,' Anna said, wistfully, 'but moving around anywhere in Germany has become next to impossible without permission, let alone going to Switzerland. If you can't give them a vital reason for travelling they just won't let you.'

'Couldn't we try going over the mountains?' Hugo asked.

'And freeze to death?' his mother said. 'Besides, the Nazis have guards on the mountain passes and in the forests. In case you hadn't noticed, the Nazis don't do things by halves. Now, listen, put your bags next to your sister's and keep everything nice and neat. The man who's coming to drive you to War School will most likely be a Nazi, which means we can't keep him waiting.'

5

Departure

The driver arrived at exactly ten o'clock that morning. He was so perfectly on time that Hugo wondered whether he hadn't waited around the corner before turning into the drive a few seconds before he was due.

He was indeed a Nazi, and indeed about as much of Nazi as you could get.

'What house have they put you in, young man?' the driver asked Hugo, once Anna had invited the driver into the house. He had blond hair, and the insignia of the SS on his shoulder. Every few seconds he would brush at the collar patch. It was obviously a point of great pride for him.

Hugo knew 'SS' was short for Schutzstaffel, the elite paramilitary organisation responsible for the concentration camps, and for so many of the terrible things the Nazis were doing in Germany and beyond.

'Hitler house, sir,' Hugo said. He wanted to keep conversation with the Nazi driver to a minimum.

'I'm glad to hear it!' the driver exclaimed. He tended to speak in exclamations. 'It's the house that breeds leaders! And you, young lady?' the driver asked, turning to Lottie. 'What house have they put you in?'

'Nuremburg house, sir,' Lottie replied carefully.

'That's also an excellent house!' the driver returned.

'My daughter loves drawing and painting,' Anna explained. 'Lottie did that watercolour over there, for example.'

The driver got to his feet and walked slowly around the room, the heels of his shiny black boots clicking against the wooden floor. He stopped beside the soft watercolour of the Safin house with its white shutters on the windows and examined it.

'This is an excellent painting!' he exclaimed.

'Thank you, sir,' said Lottie.

Neither Hugo nor Lottie had given him an answer longer than three words yet. An SS officer talking to them in such a relaxed manner was an extremely uncomfortable experience.

The man finished his coffee, drinking it down to the very last sip.

'Excellent coffee!' he exclaimed. 'So much better than the Ersatz substitute made from roast acorns. How it is you have real coffee, Mrs Safin?'

'Oh, I have a little left from before the War,' she replied. 'I only give it to special guests.'

Hugo knew his mother was trying to butter the Nazi up.

'Well, many thanks for it, Mrs Safin,' the SS officer said. 'Right, now we must depart. 'Hugo and Lottie, say goodbye to your mother.'

Anna walked up to both of her children and kissed their foreheads.

'Be careful,' she whispered.

'There's no need for you to worry about their security, Mrs Safin,' said the Nazi. 'They'll be completely safe at War School.'

Anna gave a nod but said nothing. She stayed in the doorway as her children walked to the man's car. It was a large, luxurious black Mercedes Benz.

It seemed to Hugo that the car had been designed with fear in mind. Its windows had been blacked out, the wheel arches flared, and there were two bright black and red swastika flags on the bonnet.

Lottie and Hugo packed their things into the boot and sat down in the back, leaving the front passenger seat pointedly empty.

'Be good!' Anna shouted as the car pulled out of the drive. Her children waved at her out of the window until they were out of sight of the house. Hugo propped his head on the window and watched the countryside go by.

He glanced at Lottie. 'We're going to a new life.'

Lottie nodded. She looked tearful.

'A wonderful new life, as pupils at the famous War School!' the SS driver added, in his fanatically enthusiastic voice.

6

Arrival

Hugo woke abruptly. His head had been slowly sliding down the window and it had eventually hit the curved part of the door at the foot of the window. Rubbing his head, he looked at his sister, who was eating a cheese and gherkin sandwich.

'Where'd you get that?' Hugo asked.

'Mother packed us lunch,' she said, eating up to the crust and dropping it into a paper bag next to her.

'In our bags?' Hugo asked. Lottie nodded.

'I don't suppose you got mine out when you got yours?' he asked.

'I did actually, but since you were asleep I hope you don't mind I had it as well,' Lottie said. 'I was too nervous to have more than a roll and butter for breakfast. I'm starving.'

'Great,' Hugo said humourlessly. 'What on earth am I going to eat?'

Lottie didn't reply and she kept her face placid. The Nazi driver cleared his throat. 'Being hungry is very character-building, Hugo!' he exclaimed. 'It makes a man tough and strong.'

Hugo nodded, forgetting the driver couldn't see him, not sure how to reply. When she heard the driver talk, Lottie broke out into a smile and dug out a pack of wrapped sandwiches from the foot compartment in front of her. She handed it over to her brother.

'You didn't think I'd let you starve, did you?' she said. Hugo smiled and tore the paper off, before wolfing down the first sandwich, which contained sliced hard-boiled egg and lettuce. He felt his hunger start to vanish. The driver took Hugo's silence for boredom, and so he spoke again in his Nazi drawl.

'Why don't you look outside to entertain yourselves?' the driver asked. 'Nothing should fill you with more happiness than the sight of our beautiful Fatherland, ruled by the greatest man in history, Adolf Hitler!'

'Yes sir,' Hugo said. He focused on the scenery that was passing them by. Hugo hadn't often left Cranz, the suburb of Hamburg where the Safin family lived, so these vistas of green and brown were fairly new to him.

The gorgeous, rolling hills they drove past made it hard for Hugo to understand why Germany was at war at all. What was the point of invading anywhere else when there was beauty of this calibre right on the doorstep?

He stared out at the countryside for the two hours of the journey, during which the conversation in the car had been pretty sporadic. During the journey's progress, he began to notice more cars coming past them and there seemed to be less open grassy space flanking the road. A few pedestrians saluted the car as it drove by, and their driver would tip his head to acknowledge them.

'We're a couple of minutes away from War School,' the driver announced at last.

Hugo tried to get comfortable, shaking his legs to fend off pins and needles. He looked for a sign that said War School. There weren't any.

The man turned off the main road and into a forest, the sudden darkness like the snuffing of a lamp.

A small part of Hugo's mind advised him to be alert, this man had driven them into a forest without any explanation but, at the same time, this didn't feel like the kind of forest in which bad things happened. Yes, it was dark, but just enough light filtered in to see the latter stages of autumn on the trees.

Hugo and Lottie didn't need to ask if War School was the building they were driving up to, they just knew. The car approached a magnificent country house, with brown walls and white windowpanes that contrasted with the green and yellow of the trees beautifully.

The building, a magnificent four-storey structure, was so stunning that the two of them almost neglected to notice the fountain that stood proudly in front of it, spurting water at least six metres into the air.

The car made a soft crunching noise as it drove over the bed of fine gravel surrounding the fountain. They finally came to a stop in front of War School's grand wooden doors. An ornate swastika had been engraved on the door, and the knocker was a golden eagle.

The three of them stepped out of the car and Hugo very nearly fell over, his legs stiff from travelling so long. The driver strode towards the doors, not bothering to check if Hugo and Lottie followed him. They took a second to find their feet again, and then rushed over to the doors, and as soon as they stood beside him, the man rapped the door three times with the knocker.

A porter with white gloves opened the door and let the three of them inside. He closed it behind them and, without a word, went back to standing in what was obviously his usual position to the side of the door.

The room the three of them stood in was obviously the reception. It was quiet, comfortably furnished; and an organised-looking woman, her black hair in a bun, sat behind a desk in the far corner.

There were two doors in the room. One was plain brown and matched the walls; the other was black with a small plaque that read 'Director'.

'You're right on time. The director, Mr Adolf von Ribbentrop, is in his office with your guides,' the woman paused in a very mechanic way, as if rehearsed, before continuing. 'Yes, our director shares a name with our glorious leader. You may go in.' She didn't even look up as she spoke, preferring to concentrate on her typewriter.

'Thank you,' the driver said. He turned to face Lottie and Hugo. 'This is where I leave you. Good luck! Heil Hitler!'

'Thank you for driving us,' Hugo said levelly, stowing his emotions away. The man nodded to each of them and exited the reception, only pausing to allow the porter to open the door for him.

After he'd gone, Lottie and Hugo strode towards the director's door

'Ladies first,' Hugo said, beckoning her ahead of him. Lottie stepped forward and twisted the doorknob. She meant to open it in one sweeping movement, but it was a heavy door, and she had to lean against it to make it move.

Lottie, usually so good at hiding her feelings, stood with her mouth slightly open, in awe of the grandeur of the director's office. The exterior of the building had been uniform and beautiful, with its rows of windows and perfectly symmetrical face; but the director's office was regal. The ceiling was high and several portraits and landscape paintings had been tastefully arranged around its perimeter. The carpet was far more luxurious than anything Hugo had ever walked on before, and was difficult to move through quickly.

The room was dominated by a portrait of Adolf Hitler on the wall behind the director's desk. It had been painted with the age-old artist's trick of eyes staring straight out, so wherever they stood, the man sized face seemed to be looking at them.

'Lottie! Hugo!' a plump man of about forty years smiled at them from across the room. He was wearing a black Nazi uniform.

By his sides were two boys, both dressed in what seemed to be standard attire there at War School: grey Nazi uniform. The one to the director's left was a tall, handsome boy who, Hugo thought, looked every bit the Nazi ideal, with blonde hair and blue eyes. The collars of his uniform were adorned with three silver bars and an SS insignia, all of them very shiny.

The other boy was shorter, with curly brown hair. A passer-by might think him plain, but for a very distinct glint in his green eyes, which seemed to take in every detail they chanced upon and log it for later use.

'Let me be the first to formally welcome you,' said the man, who had a deep, booming voice. 'My name is Adolf von Ribbentrop, and I am proud to be director of War School. You may have heard of the great Joachim von Ribbentrop; he is a distant relative of mine. I am also proud to have the same first name as our glorious leader. Heil Hitler!'

'Heil Hitler!' the tall blonde boy said quickly, and the shorter boy joined him for the last few syllables.

'Heil Hitler,' Hugo and Lottie said, as convincingly as they could.

Hugo had vaguely heard of Joachim von Ribbentrop: one of the very top Nazis.

Adolf von Ribbentrop pointed at the boys. 'These two fine young men are to be your guides around our fantastic facility.'

'It's beautiful,' Lottie gushed. 'We're just so happy to be here.' The director smiled.

'War School is the best training school in the German Reich,' Adolf von Ribbentrop said passionately. 'Millions of German children can only dream of coming here, but you two have been chosen to attend. At War School, your minds will be trained, nurtured, evolved and developed until they function at peak efficiency. Heil Hitler!'

The tall blonde boy had stood straight and still for the whole time the director had been talking, but the brown haired boy had started to slouch and shifting from foot to foot. The final command jolted back to attention.

Von Ribbentrop clapped his hands together. 'I have kept you here too long, and you are probably itching to see the rest of War School.'

'Should we take them there now?' the brown-haired boy asked.

'Yes, but first you must introduce yourselves to our new students,' Von Ribbentrop said, his voice now sterner. The blonde boy loosened up immediately and thrust his arm out towards Lottie.

'I'm Jens,' he said with a smile. The director gave him a look, and he sighed, 'Jens Goebbels.'

'As in...?' Lottie's eyes widened.

'Yes, Joseph Goebbels is my uncle,' Jens said tiredly. Hugo had to stop himself taking a step back in horror. How could a monster like Goebbels have such a normal-looking nephew? Lottie shook his hand calmly, and Jens beckoned her to follow him. The two of them left the room before the shorter boy had said anything; and Hugo heard Lottie say, 'I'm Lottie. Lottie Safin,' before they went beyond earshot.

Hugo watched them disappear. Lottie's eagerness to leave so quickly was, Hugo felt sure, obviously to do with Jens's looks. It was so like her, leaving him in the lurch for the sake of a boy. She was always having him wait around at school while she flirted with someone or other. But he couldn't resent her for it, she didn't do it deliberately. It was just her way.

'I'm Oliver Muller,' said the other boy, offering Hugo a hand the same way Jens had.

'Hugo Safin,' Hugo said, taking Oliver's hand, and finding it firm but friendly.

'We should get started then, it takes a quite a while to see everything,' Oliver said, leading Hugo towards the door.

Once the large wooden doors had closed behind them, Oliver relaxed visibly. The secretary wasn't at her desk any more. His sudden smile warmed Hugo to him even more.

'Is Mr von Ribbentrop strict?' asked Hugo, feeling no longer bound by Hitler's watchful eyes.

'He's strict but fair,' said Oliver shrugging. 'He's fine so long as you're not in his bad books.'

'Are you ever in his bad books?'

'I am at the moment,' said Oliver. 'In fact, I'm doing your orientation as a punishment. That probably tells you all you need to know. Is there anywhere you want to see first?'

The sandwiches had been nice but it had been a long journey. 'Could we start with the dining hall?' Hugo asked.

'Good choice,' said Oliver, and he led Hugo through the other door in the reception, the brown one.

Lottie had never been amazed so many times in one day. She was standing in the middle of a courtyard surrounded by four buildings. The largest and most beautiful was the main building she'd just left, but three worthy competitors to that title stood on the opposite side.

Jens had taken her to every little bit of the main building; the classrooms, which made the ones at her old school in Cranz look ugly and impractical; the hall, where, Jens said, assemblies were held and Sunday dinners were eaten; and the assortment of exquisitely tasteful rooms that seemed to her to serve no purpose but to remind students of War School's past life as a country house.

'What are they for?' Lottie asked, pointing at the three other buildings in the courtyard.

'The building in the middle accommodates Hitler house, and those over there are the buildings for Nuremburg and Fatherland house,' Jens said. 'The one on the left is Nuremburg and the one on the right is Fatherland.'

'Where's Victory house?' Lottie asked.

'About half a kilometre out into the forest,' Jens said. 'They need the space for the sports they do, and it means that stray bullets from the firing range are less likely to hit someone.'

'There's a firing range?' Lottie asked, genuinely impressed.

'Yes, of course, this is War School, after all!' Jens said. 'Everything is paid for by the government. They want us to have the best facilities possible.'

'What house are you in?' Lottie asked.

'Hitler house,' he said, pointing to the three-bars on his collar.

Each bar had a small letter H engraved on it, H being the first letter of Hitler, Lottie guessed.

'The bars are a kind of rank,' Jens explained. 'I have three-bars, which makes me one of only five three-bar students in my house.'

'So you're pretty high up then?' Lottie asked.

'Yes, the only person above me is the sole four-bar of the house.'

'That's good. I like to have friends in high places,' Lottie said. Jens laughed.

'I'll show you the lake now,' Jens said after he had stopped laughing. 'It's right behind the house buildings.'

Lottie looked carefully; she could see bits of blue in the gaps between them.

'That sounds nice,' Lottie said. The two of them started walking.

'I forgot to ask, what do the other houses do for ranking?' Lottie said.

'Everyone uses bars, in Hitler house we have a small H in the middle of ours, in Nuremburg house there's an N, and so on,' Jens said.

'I see,' Lottie said, and she and Jens walked towards the lake in a pleasant, companionable silence.

7

Andrea

To get from the reception to the dining hall at War School, you had to go past most of the rooms in the main building. Oliver showed them to Hugo as they went by.

Oliver seemed to be quite a popular boy; everyone they met in the hallways greeted him and asked who Hugo was.

After a time, they approached an ominous set of swastika-adorned doors. Grinning, Oliver pushed them open to reveal a cavernous dining hall, empty at the minute but with tables set for an elaborate meal. The ceiling was impressively high and a beautiful chandelier hung from it, each of its crystals sparkling like cat's eyes.

'What's the food here like?' Hugo asked.

'Pretty good,' Oliver said, 'they work us hard, but they feed us well, too.' Hugo followed him to a line serve that was an ugly reminder that they were in a dining hall. Oliver got two trays and gave one to Hugo.

'Why are you two so late to lunch?' the young man in a white apron behind the line serve looked at the two of them suspiciously.

'Orientation,' Oliver said.

'Ah,' the man said, as though that one word explained anything, 'So, what do you want then?'

'Sour cabbage and braised pork, please,' Oliver said immediately. The young man nodded and started to dish Oliver's food onto a plate for him.

'What about you, Hugo?' Oliver asked. Hugo thought of his mother and how she was possibly the best cook in the world. She mostly cooked Russian meals at home, of course using German ingredients.

'I don't really mind what I eat,' Hugo said.

'You can have what I'm having then,' Oliver said.

'Oh... actually, I'm not really in a pork mood,' Hugo said, measuring his tone so as to sound unsuspicious. 'Is there anything else?' he asked politely. Being Jewish, Hugo had obviously never eaten pork before, and had long before decided that he would not give up his faith completely for his family's cover.

The man looked up and down, opening cupboards.

'There are a couple of chicken sandwiches here from lunch...' he began, but Hugo cut him off immediately, not wanting to draw suspicion to himself by being fussy.

'That sounds great. Thank you,' Hugo said, trying not to show his relief. The man looked confused as he handed them two plates.

Hugo and Oliver sat at the same table, they both had a lot of food on their plates. They are quickly and quietly, and finished eating at about the same time.

'Should we take our plates back?' Hugo asked, getting to his feet.

'You don't have to,' Oliver said, cleaning around his mouth with a napkin, 'but if you are, could you take mine?' Hugo smiled and took Oliver's plate along with his. He piled the two plates onto a rack that held a few other dirty dishes and nodded at the young man behind the line serve, who looked pointedly at the plates, not enthusiastic about having two more to clean.

'Thanks,' Oliver said when Hugo returned.

'What are we doing now?' Hugo asked.

Oliver looked down at his watch. 'It's one thirty. Jens should've finished showing your sister around now. They better hurry up if they want any lunch! Let's go and meet them before you go to your houses.'

'Where did you arrange to meet?' Hugo asked as Oliver led him out.

'The courtyard behind the main building,' Oliver said.

There seemed to be more students in the building than before, so Oliver and Hugo had to swerve and move in the hallways to avoid walking into them, but soon the two of them walked out into the sunshine of the courtyard. Oliver looked around, trying to spot Jens's blonde hair among the crowds of students.

'Can you see them?' Hugo asked.

'No,' Oliver said, 'Jens isn't usually late for anything.' The two of them waited a while longer before Hugo saw two laughing figures approach them.

'Isn't that them there?' Hugo said pointing towards the two figures. Oliver looked where Hugo pointed and nodded.

'Yes,' Oliver said. 'Why are they both so shiny?' Hugo hadn't given much thought to it before, but the sun was shining off the two of them in a very odd way. The answer became clearer as they came closer – they were soaking wet.

'What happened?' Oliver asked, as soon as they were within speaking distance.

'She pushed me into the lake!' Jens said. 'The water was freezing!' But he had a wide smile on his face.

'You said Nuremburg house was pointless!' Lottie said.

'Drawing maps isn't hard!' Jens retorted.

'Hold on, Lottie,' Hugo interjected, 'if you pushed him in, why are you wet as well?'

Jens and Lottie looked at each other and broke into a new round of laughter.

'After she pushed me in, she came to the lakeside to gloat,' Jens said, 'So I grabbed her leg and pulled her in as well.' Lottie gave Jens a superficial punch on the arm before turning to her brother.

'What have you done since we got here then?' she asked.

'I had lunch,' Hugo said. Lottie twisted her hair to squeeze the water out before she replied to her brother.

'You ate on the way here!' she said. Hugo shrugged.

'I was still a bit hungry when we arrived,' he said. Lottie tutted and shook her head.

'Being hungry is character building for a young man, you know!' she said in an effective parody of their former driver's passionate Nazi outburst.

'Oh, ha ha,' said Hugo. Oliver looked at the two of them and decided he didn't want to know.

'I won't ask what that's all about,' Oliver said. 'Lottie, I think I should take you to Nuremburg house, to show you around.'

'I was going to take her,' Jens said.

'Wouldn't it make sense for you to take Hugo?' Oliver asked. 'You're in Hitler house with him after all.'

'Yes, it would make sense, wouldn't it?' Jens said, already walking off with Lottie in tow.

'They seem to have hit it off pretty quickly,' Oliver commented, as he led Hugo towards the Hitler house building. It was between two slightly smaller buildings and seemed the busiest of the houses, with students coming in and out constantly.

A student leaving the building held the door open for them. When it closed behind them it shut out all the noise of the courtyard.

Hugo and Oliver stood in a short hallway with two doors on each side. The doors were made of a dark wood that complemented the maroon walls perfectly.

'Ahem,' someone behind them stage coughed. It was a girl with a hockey stick slung over her shoulder. Even in the softly lit corridor, Hugo could tell that she was stunningly pretty. Her straight, dark hair caressed her shoulders, and her brown eyes sparked with resolve.

Now her eyes narrowed on Oliver.

'Andrea!' Oliver said, 'I didn't see you there.'

'Well, now you have,' she said, wryly. 'What are you doing here?' And who's that?' she asked, nodding towards Hugo.

'A new student, and I'm doing his orientation,' Oliver replied.

Andrea appeared to relax after hearing that, and put a hand out for Hugo to shake.

'And you are…?' Andrea said. It took Hugo a few moments to realise she was talking to him. Oliver gave him a nudge and he focused with a start. Andrea laughed and Hugo went red.

'Hugo Safin,' he said, shaking Andrea's hand.

'Pleased to meet you, Hugo. I'm Andrea Ducasse,' she replied. 'My grandfather on my father's side was born in France,' she added, to explain her surname. 'Well, it's nice to meet you, Hugo,' Andrea said, retracting her hand gently from his too-long grasp. Hugo tried to reply but he found that he could only manage a nod. There was a smirk on her face as she walked past them and towards the staircase at the end of the hallway.

Hugo started to follow her, but Oliver held him until her footsteps had faded. They both moved against the wall to let a student go by.

'Good first impression,' he said, as they went up the stairs.

If the dining hall was like a restaurant, Hugo thought, the second floor of Hitler house looked and felt like a hotel.

Brown seemed to be the colour of choice here; the doors of the students' rooms were all mahogany, with a shiny brass number and a varying number of silver bars on them. The floor underfoot was a thick, rich carpet. Hitler house went up a few more floors, and they all seemed to be as lavish as this one.

'Your room's number sixteen,' Oliver said, walking Hugo to his door. Hugo skated his hand on the wooden rail that guarded the drop onto the stairs.

'How do you know what my room number is?' Hugo asked.

'The director told me in his office,' Oliver said, producing a key from his pocket and twisting it in the lock of door sixteen, which Hugo noticed had no bars on it.

Hugo's new room was larger than the one at his house, and the bed was a luxurious looking four-poster. The desk in the room was even next to the window, just the way Hugo liked it.

Everything looked good until he turned a corner and saw what was facing the bed: a painting – about a metre from top to bottom and half a metre wide - of Hitler. Hugo had a feeling that his dark, searching eyes would be the first and last things he saw every day.

He wrenched his eyes away from the painting and turned to face Oliver, who was studying him with interest.

'Where's the toilet?' Hugo asked.

'It's through there,' Oliver said, pointing at a white door to the right of the painting. Hugo muttered a thank you and headed for the bathroom, avoiding eye contact with the country's leader.

Hugo didn't actually need the lavatory; but he locked the door behind him and looked at his face in the mirror. He looked as nervous as he felt, with deep creases on his forehead. He took a few deep breaths and it felt like he was relaxing a bit, but the thought of the painting outside brought the creases right back onto his face.

A knock on the door made him jump.

'Hugo? Are you all right?' Oliver asked.

'One second,' Hugo said quickly. A moment or two later he flushed the lavatory, and waited a few moments longer before leaving the bathroom, shutting the door behind him.

Oliver was standing a respectful distance away from the door, waiting.

'Your room's a little smaller than mine,' he mused half to himself, looking around. Hugo walked around him and sat on the bed, with his back to the portrait.

'So what do you think? Oliver asked.

'Of what?' Hugo asked.

'Of this place, War School,' Oliver said.

Hugo thought for a second, what did he think of War School? The whole place was extraordinary, amazing even, and of course terrible too. He knew he would never feel completely at ease here. He tried telling himself that he was in a normal place full of normal people, but the fact that Oliver was dressed in SS uniform kept reminding him he was in a school designed to train killers.

'It's great,' was all Hugo said, diplomatically. Oliver snorted and paced around the room.

'I didn't think you were that gullible,' he said to himself.

'Pardon?' Hugo asked. Oliver didn't repeat himself; instead, he turned to face Hugo, looking him straight in the eye.

'Do you think we're going to win this war?' he asked.

'Yes, of course I do,' Hugo replied automatically. If Oliver was trying to trick him then he would have to try harder than that, Hugo thought.

'Well I don't,' Oliver said quickly and quietly, 'and if you ask me, this place is just breeding people to pick up the pieces when we lose.'

Hugo felt as if the words had been burning a hole in Oliver's mind and they had seared their way down to his tongue. Hugo knew that if an SS officer had overheard Oliver say what he'd just said, Oliver would have almost certainly been executed, that very day, by the SS officer taking him out into the nearby forest and shooting him in the back of the neck. Any talk of defeat for Nazi Germany was regarded as pure treason.

A smile crept onto the curly-haired boy's face.

'You agree with me!' he said happily.

'How do you know?' Hugo asked.

'I just do. I can tell.'

Hugo didn't say anything.

'I knew I couldn't be the only person with some sense in this country!' Oliver exclaimed.

'What would you have done if I hadn't agreed with you?' Hugo took a chance and asked Oliver, who still wore a massive grin.

'Pretended it was a test or something,' Oliver said instantly, 'When did you realise the truth?'

'Well, my mother hasn't trusted the Nazis since they came into power,' Hugo said quickly. If Oliver was suspicious, he didn't show it. He was walking towards a large closet that stood in the corner furthest away from the door.

'You'll love this then,' Oliver pulled the closet open, and inside were five full sets of grey Nazi uniform. At the top was a military style cap next to what Hugo assumed was athletic kit. There was even a chic little shelf for the red, swastika-adorned armbands.

'Do we wear the uniform everywhere in the school?' Hugo asked.

'Apart from when we're doing sports... or you get lucky with a girl!' Oliver said, 'which reminds me, we don't wear them in bed either.'

'I'll keep that in mind,' Hugo said with a smile.

'I'll leave you to unpack,' Oliver said, 'see you at dinner this evening then.'

'See you then, Oliver,' Hugo said, 'and thanks for showing me around.'

'My pleasure,' Oliver replied.

About half an hour after Oliver left; Hugo looked tiredly around his room and was finally satisfied he could live in this space. He had unpacked all of his clothes and put them away neatly, something he'd hardly ever done before and was surprised to find himself enjoying.

The biggest change, however, was on the wall opposite the bed. Hugo had taken out the nail that held the painting of Hitler up, and after spending ages trying to find a position out of Hitler's line of sight. Hugo knew that it would be stupid – even maybe suicidal – to take the Führer's portrait down, but after a while he managed to put the nail about half a metre higher, knocking it in with the sole of his right shoe. He then put the portrait back up, and Hugo now found that the great leader was too high up for Hitler's gaze to be on Hugo all the time, which suited Hugo perfectly. He was much more comfortable without the Führer watching his every move.

Hugo was just taking the last of his books from his bag when there was a knock at the door.

'Hugo Safin?' a girl's voice sounded behind the door. Hugo moved to open it quickly and was surprised to find Andrea there in the doorway.

'Um... hello?' Hugo said nervously.

'May I come in?' she asked politely. Hugo was hardly going to refuse, and he opened the door wider so she could.

Hugo's eyes were drawn to the four silver bars on the collar of her grey uniform as she walked past him.

'So...' Hugo started, not knowing how to phrase his question.

'Why am I here?' Andrea suggested. Hugo smiled.

'Yeah,' Hugo said thankfully. It wasn't a very polite thing to ask and he was glad he hadn't had to.

'I'm the four-bar of Hitler house, so I'm required to meet every new student we get,' Andrea explained. She took one look at Hugo's blank face and sighed, 'Oliver hasn't explained properly what four bar means, has he?'

'Should he have?' Hugo asked.

'I shouldn't have expected him to,' Andrea said. She looked down at her watch and then back up at Hugo, 'I'll summarise quickly then.' She thought for a second before she began. 'Everyone at War School has a rank, and you can tell what rank someone is by the number of silver bars on their collar. The lowest rank is a no bar, like you are now.'

'Thanks,' Hugo said. Andrea laughed.

'You won't be one for long, no-one ever is,' she said.

'How do I get a bar?' Hugo asked.

'You get your first bar by taking part in your first battle,' Andrea said.

'When you say battle, do you mean a war game in the woods or something?' Hugo asked

'Yeah, exactly like that,' Andrea said, 'we work with Victory house and run mock battles in the woods.'

'How does that work?' Hugo asked, 'surely we don't shoot bullets at each other?'

Andrea shrugged. 'Yes, of course. It keeps numbers down,' she said.

Hugo looked alarmed before he realised she was joking.

'Had you for a second,' she said, with a smile.

'For a second,' Hugo conceded. 'So how does it actually work?'

'We shoot little paint filled-pellet things,' Andrea said, 'when they hit you they burst and you get a splatter of paint on you. That means you're dead. We wear goggles so we don't get the pellets in our eyes.'

'I see. So, to get my first bar, I'd need to take part in one of these battles?'

Andrea nodded.

'How do I get my second bar?' Hugo asked.

'You get your second bar once you've performed well in five battles.' Andrea replied.

'Who decides if I've performed well?' asked Hugo.

'The director, Mr von Ribbentrop.'

'Oh, him,' said Hugo. 'Yes, I've met him. But what about the third and fourth bars? How do you get those?'

'That's a bit more complicated,' Andrea said. 'We keep track of the number of battles every student in Hitler house participates in. The person who's taken part in the most battles is awarded four bars.'

'Which is you,' Hugo said.

Andrea nodded. 'Exactly. At the moment, at least. The next five students below the four bar are awarded three-bars.'

'Do I have to salute every time I see you or something?' Hugo asked, only half joking.

'Now that you mention it, I wouldn't half mind,' Andrea mused, 'perhaps you could do a little bow as well,' she said. Hugo laughed, and as he did, Andrea got to her feet and looked around his room.

'What is it?' he asked.

'Are you any good...' she dipped her hand inside Hugo's open suitcase and came up with a chessboard, 'at this?'

'I'm OK,' Hugo said modestly.

'Chess is an important game here at War School,' Andrea explained, 'our director, Adolf von Ribbentrop, was a keen player when he was younger, and he believes that chess perfectly complements the lessons we have in Hitler house.'

'Makes sense,' Hugo said, nodding.

'I'd give you a game, but I...' Andrea slapped her forehead, 'I completely forgot! I'm late for a meeting!' She looked apologetic as she turned towards the door to leave.

'Andrea?' Hugo asked, just before she crossed the threshold.

'Yes?' she said, turning around.

'It was nice meeting you,' Hugo said.

'Nice meeting you too,' she said, giving him a radiant smile as she left. Hugo stared at the door for a long while after her footsteps had faded.

8

First Day

Hugo woke whilst it was still dark outside. He had slept badly, waking up every few hours from familiar and vivid nightmares.

The mere thought of leaving his bed sent warning shivers up his spine, and his brain came up with every possible excuse for not moving. Through force of will and the thought of arriving to his first lesson late, he managed to lift himself upright and throw the duvet off his legs.

Hugo plodded slowly to the bathroom, rubbing his eyes and yawning the whole way there. He tried to shake the sleep from his head. He'd need to be more alert for his first day. He washed quickly, then splashed his face, but when he came out, he realised he would have to put on one of the grey uniforms in the wardrobe.

Choosing to do it rather than think about it, Hugo took the uniform from the hanger and put it on.

His mother must have sent them his sizes because everything fit perfectly, and the dark boots were like socks on his feet.

A full-sized mirror in the door of the wardrobe told Hugo exactly what he didn't need to be told: He looked like a Nazi - the image of his lifelong fear. As he pulled on the red armband, he decided that he needed to talk to his sister. She was definitely dealing with this better than he was, and as much as he didn't want to admit it, he could use some empathy.

Hugo walked out of his room and a quick look around told him that there was no one about. He looked around at the doors on his floor, and he saw that there was no one ranked above one-bar on this level. This wasn't the top floor though, and Hugo assumed those with two-bars or more slept on the level above.

He was paying so little attention to his surroundings that he didn't see Jens plod up the stairs and approach him. Jens was red-faced and he wore a sports kit. His skin was covered in a thin sheen of sweat.

'Good morning, Hugo!' Jens exclaimed, 'I've just finished my morning run, really cold this morning, you know.'

'Yes, I'm sure it was,' Hugo said. He couldn't fail to notice that Jens was an impressive physical specimen, even by the standards of War School. He was tall, broad and perfectly muscled. Standing in front of him, Hugo couldn't help but feel a bit inferior.

'Sleep well?' Jens asked.

'Yes, very well thanks,' Hugo said.

'Sorry about yesterday,' Jens said, his cheeks reddening even more, 'I started off showing your sister around so I thought I might as well finish, nothing personal.'

'Don't worry about it,' Hugo said. He had very much wanted Jens to be a horrible, cruel person, in view of who Jens's uncle was, but there was an honesty and kindness in his voice that Hugo hadn't expected.

'Having breakfast?' Jens asked.

'Definitely, I'm starving,' Hugo said.

'I'll just go and change quickly, wait right here!' Jens shot up the stairs to the second floor and was back within five minutes, uniform perfectly neat and his hair tidy.

'Come on then,' he said. Hugo followed him down the stairs and onto the bottom floor of Hitler house, where students were either milling about or heading towards the dining hall. They walked past two imposing black doors. Hugo eyed them curiously. Jens noticed Hugo look at the doors, and stopped walking.

'They're the strategy rooms,' Jens explained, 'follow me,' he opened the heavy doors and they went in.

It was a large, long, wood-panelled room. The far wall was covered in a map of the world with Germany, and the territories it controlled, in red.

'Do they change the map to include recent advances?' Hugo asked as they surveyed the room below them.

'Yes, every day we get someone from Nuremburg house to check the map and update it,' Jens said proudly.

'What happens if we go back?' Hugo asked.

'What do you mean?' Jens replied.

'If they... I mean, if we have to retreat for some reason?' Hugo asked. Jens laughed and put a strong arm around Hugo's shoulder.

'Don't be ridiculous Hugo,' Jens said, with a confident smile. 'The army of the Fatherland never retreats, or loses.'

'What about the Battle of Britain?' Hugo said.

Jens's smile faltered a little and his eyes darkened a lot.

'We should never have started a bombing campaign in Britain so early in the war,' he said, 'the officer in charge of the operation said it would take four days, but it almost took four months and still we lost! As for the British, they are persistent and stubborn devils, but what do you expect from people living on an island?'

'Why didn't anyone from War School say something to German High Command?' Hugo asked. Jens laughed a harsher laugh this time.

'And openly oppose the senior Nazis?' Jens asked, 'the last time someone did that they were expelled from the Nazi party and sent to Dachau for six months, which many regarded as quite lenient treatment compared to what could have happened. Jens looked down at his watch, 'if we leave now, we could still get a late breakfast.'

'Sounds good,' Hugo said, but all he could really think of was how despicable the Nazis were.

The dining hall had a relaxed atmosphere during breakfast; students came and went irregularly, although a few groups of friends sat down to enjoy the most important meal of the day together.

The larger boys, that Hugo assumed were from Victory house, ate off plates stacked high with food.

'What do you fancy?' Jens asked as the two of them approached the line serve. There was no one behind it – the food was all on the counter for them to take themselves, 'Dutch cheese? Fried eggs? Bacon? Sausages? Devilled kidneys? The devilled kidneys - lambs' kidneys cooked with mustard and cayenne pepper - are really delicious; it's amazing there's any left!'

Hugo had never tried a sausage, German sausages being made from pork, but he was sorely tempted by the sight of the perfectly browned meat stacked in a pyramid on the counter.

'I'll have a few rolls and some fried eggs,' Hugo said, taking an empty plate and filling it himself.

'Jam?' Jens offered, 'it's from France, yet another German conquest!' he added enthusiastically. Hugo nodded and accepted the pot from his friend, before lathering on the inside of his rolls.

'Go and find somewhere to sit,' Jens said, 'I'll be there in a second,' Hugo chose a table close to the door and sat down.

He was about half way through his meal when Jens finally arrived.

'You took your time,' he said.

'I'm bigger than you so I have to eat more!' Jens exclaimed, setting his extravagantly laden plate down. 'Besides, I've just worked up an appetite with a run.'

He ate in a very organised way – first the eggs, then the cheese, and finally the bacon with the sausages. He looked up as he swallowed the butt of a sausage.

'You didn't have any meat,' Jens said, puzzled.

'I didn't feel like it this morning,' Hugo said quickly.

'Didn't feel like sausages?' Jens asked, trying to find some reason in what he had just heard.

'Yes, that's right,' Hugo replied. Jens struggled with the idea for another moment before shrugging.

'Suit yourself,' he said.

When the last rasher of bacon had disappeared down Jens's gullet, he rose from the table and cleaned his mouth with a napkin.

'Come on then,' Jens said, 'don't want you to be late to your first lesson.' They left their plates and strode out of the dining hall. A shout made them look around as the dining hall's doors closed behind them.

'Jens!' Hugo and Jens both looked for the source of the yell, and Hugo spotted a very familiar shade of blonde hair coming towards them.

'Hello Lottie,' Jens said, 'where are you off to this morning?'

'The woods,' Lottie said, 'I have a test of some sort. Wish me luck!' and with that, she turned and blended into the stream of people heading towards the front doors.

Jens led Hugo to the right. The sea of students the two of them had been walking through thinned to a stream as they went on.

'Morning, Jens,' a boy's voice said. He was walking in the same direction they were, and the collar of his grey jacket had three-bars on it.

'Good morning,' Jens replied, not bothering to look over.

'Who's that?' the boy asked. He took a step over and inspected Hugo's collar, 'Ah. New boy.' he said with distaste.

Jens nodded and carried on walking.

'What's your name, new boy?' the stranger asked abruptly.

'Hugo Safin,' Hugo said, copying Jens's example and continuing to walk. There was a short, impatient silence before the boy spoke again.

'Aren't you going to ask my name?' he asked.

Hugo opened his mouth to defend himself, but he was too late.

'I'm Frederick Koenig!' the boy said angrily. He had started to reply before Hugo had spoken, and his expression went from patronising to furious, 'You can't talk to me like that!' he yelled. He took hold of Hugo's arm, stopping their progress down the hallway.

'Calm down, Frederick,' Jens said. A few of the students in Hitler house were staring at the three of them as they went by, 'you didn't mean it did you Hugo?' Jens asked.

'No, Frederick,' Hugo said. Frederick reluctantly let go of Hugo's arm and the three of them kept walking.

After a few seconds, Jens stopped outside a door. 'Is this our classroom?' Hugo asked.

'Nope,' Jens said. 'Shortcut,' he pushed the door open. Hugo followed him in but Frederick looked at him, shocked.

'We're not allowed to use the lounge rooms to get to lessons,' he said

'Don't give me that, I saw you go through one at lunch on Thursday,' Jens said, 'and I'm not even using it, just passing through,' Frederick looked a little embarrassed, but he put his nose into the air and walked down the hallway, rather than follow Jens.

'What is he talking about?' Hugo asked. They were moving at a noticeably quicker pace through the room than they had through the hallway.

'You know how this building used to be a country house?' Jens said.

'No, but carry on,' Hugo said.

'Well it was,' Jens said, 'and even after all of the rooms that we needed had been converted into classrooms, there were still far too many. No one saw any point in clearing them, so they were kept as the last owner of the house had left them,' Jens added, 'students can use them on weekends and after school, but not as shortcuts and especially not as places to eat lunch.'

It sounded like one of a set of rules that Jens had been told several times, and there was something, other than the fact that they were in one of these surplus rooms now, that made Hugo suspect Jens didn't pay those rules much attention.

The door on the other side of the room opened into another hallway, and a few steps to the left was an open door.

'Is this our classroom?' Hugo asked. Jens nodded and strode inside.

It looked like a lecture hall, with tiered seats that went up several rows and curved slightly around a platform at the bottom.

Most of the seats were filled, and a glance around the room told Hugo that Frederick hadn't arrived yet.

'Go and find someone to sit with,' Jens said, 'you need to meet some of the other people in the house,' Jens chose a seat close to the front, next to a boy with red hair.

Hugo looked for a friendly face and was relieved to see Andrea in the middle of the fifth row. He made his way up the steps that ran down the side of the room.

'Is anyone sitting there?' Hugo asked. Andrea had been deep in conversation with a boy sitting behind her, but she broke off immediately when she heard Hugo.

'I don't think so,' she said.

'Can I...' Hugo started. Andrea rolled her eyes.

'Go right ahead, Hugo,' she said with a smile, 'I don't think you've met Michael yet, have you?' Hugo shook his head and the boy on the row above, a lean looking boy with black hair and sharp, angular features, stuck out a hand.

'Michael Bauer, pleased to meet you,' he said politely. He was another three-bar, but right away, Hugo could tell that Michael didn't seem to be anywhere near as arrogant as Frederick was.

'When does our lesson start?' Hugo asked the two of them. Michael looked down at his watch.

'Any minute now...' Michael said. At that moment a short man – and maybe fifty years old, Hugo thought - in black SS uniform strode into the giant classroom and set a stack of papers down on the table at the front.

'Good morning, students!' he said. 'Heil Hitler!'

'Heil Hitler!' the students thundered back.

'We have a new student, Hugo Safin, in the class,' the SS teacher announced. 'Safin, welcome to the school!'

'Thank you,' Hugo said.

'My name is Herr Karl Ritter, but you will call me "sir".'

'Yes, of course, sir.' Hugo replied.

'Now,' Ritter said, 'chess boards out everyone and start an unranked chess game against your neighbour.'

The students in the room opened up the desks in front of them and produced chessboards. Behind them, Michael stopped leaning over and began to place pieces onto the board that the boy next to him had taken out.

'What's going on?' Hugo asked.

'Didn't you hear him?' she asked, 'we're playing chess.'

'Is that the lesson?' Hugo asked.

'It could be, I'm not sure,' she said. 'Things vary a lot lesson-wise. Halfway through the games he might suddenly start teaching us.' Hugo saw Andrea take a small wooden box out from under the desk that ran in front of them and started to set up the pieces. He would be playing her.

Hugo took the white ones out of the box and set them down. Setting a chessboard up and putting the pieces on the right squares was pretty much an automatic movement for him, so he allowed his mind to wonder. It wondered exactly half a metre to his left, and stayed there.

Andrea placed the small wooden pieces onto the board quickly, but each of them landed perfectly in the middle of the little squares. Hugo was completely aware he was watching Andrea a little too intently, but he couldn't help it and he wouldn't stop if he could.

'Hugo? Are you going to move?' Andrea asked.

'Oh, right,' Hugo said, relieved that she hadn't noticed him staring at her. He pushed a white pawn forward and they began to play.

It became very clear, very quickly, that Andrea was far better at chess than Lottie was. Moves that would have confused or tricked his sister didn't faze Andrea at all, and she gave a small chuckle as she countered some of them.

As the game went on, Hugo gained the upper hand; and after a few tense minutes, Andrea made a lazy move and Hugo pressed his attack. She shrugged and resigned the game a few moves before he could checkmate her.

'Good game,' she said insincerely. Losing seemed to be the one thing that Andrea did without grace, and Hugo felt slightly guilty for beating her.

'If it means anything, you're the best chess-player I've played against,' Hugo said.

'Thanks,' she said with a hint of sarcasm. 'Jens is going to be unbearable now.'

'Why am I going to be unbearable?' Jens had heard his name from three rows in front of them and turned his head.

'Never mind,' Andrea said, far too quickly for Jens to not be interested.

'No, what is it?' Jens got up out of his seat and shook hands with the red-headed boy who it seemed he had just beaten.

When Jens arrived at their desk, he looked down at the board only briefly and gave Hugo a sympathetic look.

'Unlucky, Hugo, it looks like you made a solid effort,' Jens said, 'she's the four bar of our house for a reason I guess.' Andrea was starting to go from angry to irritated, and she didn't look like correcting Jens any time soon.

'Actually, if you look harder at the position, you'll see I beat Andrea,' Hugo said. He wasn't sure what he expected Jens to do, but he definitely hadn't seen him break out into tears of laughter.

'Are you serious?' he asked, grinning ear to ear. Hugo paused mid nod when Andrea shot him a look of pure venom.

'Oh, get over yourself Andrea,' Jens said. 'I'm sure he beat you fair and square.' The three of them were silent before

Jens continued, 'you are aware though, that if we were playing ranked games...'

'Yes of course I am,' Andrea said, her face going red.

'What are you talking about?' Hugo asked.

'You remember how Mr Ritter said "unranked" chess games?' Jens asked. Hugo nodded, 'well, unranked games are like a friendly, there's nothing at stake. Ranked games are a little different.'

'In what way?' Hugo asked.

'If you lose to someone with a lower rank than you, then you swap ranks,' Andrea had spoken this time, and she looked to have calmed down at least a little.

'Ah,' Hugo said.

'Jens!' Ritter had noticed Jens's absence from his seat and yelled his name across the room. He may have been a short man, but his voice carried well enough for Jens to wince five rows away.

'Sorry sir,' Jens went back to his seat quickly, giving Hugo a nod and Andrea a parting smirk.

'Right!' Ritter said, clapping his hands together, 'if you haven't finished playing yet, stop. Give me your results at the end of the lesson.'

'Will you tell him the results, or should I?' Hugo asked, copying Jens's smile. Andrea gave him a soft punch on the arm.

'When lessons are done today, we're playing again,' she whispered. Hugo had a sneaking suspicion that she wouldn't stop playing him until she won.

'Now listen, everyone,' Ritter said. 'Earlier today, the Third Panzer Army got to within two hundred kilometres of Moscow, but due to various factors outside his control, Field Marshall Fedor von Bock is considering halting the advance.'

'Who's von Bock?' Hugo whispered to Andrea. She turned to face him.

'Seriously?' she asked. Hugo shook his head, and she sighed, 'I can't believe you beat me at chess.'

'No, I really don't know who he is,' Hugo said.

'He's in charge of army group centre,' Andrea whispered. Hugo continued to look at her blankly. 'You are at least aware that we're at war with the Russians at the moment, right?'

'I know that,' Hugo replied, 'I'm not an idiot.' The way she said 'Russians' hurt Hugo a little inside, the tone of her voice made it very clear she thought of them as the enemy.

'Well our men are split into army groups north, south and centre; so Fedor von Bock is one of the three most powerful people in the eastern front,' Andrea said.

'Should I know that?' Hugo asked warily.

'Perhaps not, but you do now,' Andrea said. Mr Ritter clapped and the room went silent instantly.

'So,' Ritter went on, 'the situation on the Russian front is getting worse and our progress has slowed considerably. Can anyone give me an example of a similar situation?'

'A similar situation in the past, sir?' a boy at the back asked.

'Well, Carsten, I think you'd struggle to give me any from the future so let's stick to the past, shall we?' A low snigger went around the room.

A few seconds passed before Hugo, keen to make a good impression at his new school, stuck his hand up.

'Sir?' he ventured.

'Ah the new boy. Yes, Safin?'

'What about Napoleon's invasion of Russia in, um...' Hugo had only planned this far, and he couldn't recall a date.

'Eighteen-twelve,' Andrea whispered to him.

'Thanks,' Hugo whispered back, 'Napoleon's invasion of Russia in eighteen-twelve.'

'Why do you mention that?' Ritter asked. His expression gave nothing away, and Hugo was wary of the fact that he might not be right.

'Um... well, because the weather's bad over at the Russian front at the moment,' Hugo said.

'As it is all year round,' Mr Ritter said.

'But it's the rasputitsa now, isn't it?' Hugo said.

'How on earth do you know that?' Ritter asked.

Hugo's mother had told him several times that every year, during the spring and autumn rasputitsa, the roads would become impossible to traverse and the ground would become a bog.

'I read it in a book,' Hugo said. Ritter nodded, looking at Hugo's face slightly quizzically.

'Well, Safin, you are completely correct. Both Napoleon's grande armée and our soldiers had, and have to, deal with the rasputitsa, which is a Russian season during which the ground becomes a quagmire. Very well done, Safin.' Ritter looked around at the class, 'before you go for break, I would like you to tell me what you would have our men do in the current difficult military situation.'

Andrea put her hand up immediately.

'Yes?' Ritter said.

'I would abandon the machinery and retreat,' she said.

Ritter looked astonished.

'Retreat?' he said.

'Otherwise they're all going to die,' she said.

'That is disgraceful defeatism, Miss Ducasse!' Ritter exclaimed.

'Sorry about that sir,' Andrea said, 'but perhaps we ought to think about our soldier's health a little more.'

'A retreat is still a retreat!' Ritter retorted, his voice now a shout. 'Anyone else have a more courageous suggestion?'

'I think we should continue to advance,' Frederick said. 'When this rasputitsa ends, the ground will harden. That'll make it easier for our tanks.'

'And winter will have started,' Andrea added.

'But they would be able to move the machines,' Frederick said, turning in his chair to face Andrea.

She was about to retort when Ritter raised his hand to silence the two of them.

'Have your argument elsewhere,' he said. He was presumably about to ask for any other ideas, but a bell cut him off.

There was an orderly rush to get to the door.

'So what is there to do at break?' Hugo asked Andrea.

'The dining hall is open, so you could get something to eat,' she said.

'I'm all right,' he said. They left the room and Andrea took him through the same shortcut that Jens had, but unlike Jens, Andrea's step didn't quicken at all.

'Oh, I forgot to ask,' she said as they came out on the other side, 'how are you finding it here?' Hugo had a feeling that she wasn't expecting the same answer that Oliver had, so he stuck to the official line.

'It's amazing,' he said with a broad smile.

'In what way?' Andrea asked.

'In every way I guess. If this morning was anything to go by, then the lessons are great too,' he said.

'I'm glad,' Andrea said. The two of them took the stairs down and left the building, stepping out into the courtyard. 'A few months ago,' Andrea said, 'we had this boy, Peter…'

'And?'

'Well, he was extraordinarily well off. According to him, if the Kaiser was still in power, he would be twelfth in line for the throne,' she paused, 'at any rate, every single day he was here, he moaned about how bad the food was and how small the rooms were.'

'What happened to him?' Hugo asked.

Andrea shrugged. 'No one really knows. One of the teachers overheard him badmouthing the school and he was gone without a trace the next morning.'

'I'm happy to be here then,' Hugo said, some genuine worry creeping into his expression. Andrea caught sight of him and laughed.

'Don't worry, I'm not going to get you into trouble if you say what you think,' Andrea said.

The two of them came to a stop close to the fountain in the middle of the courtyard. Hugo noticed that there were students going around the side of the main building, and he pointed it out to Andrea.

'What's going on?' he asked her. She looked over at the corner of the building he was pointing at.

'Let's go and see,' Andrea said.

A crowd of the kind that every schoolboy and girl is familiar with had formed on the corner of the main block. There was a tense edge to the collected students, and the majority of them were looking up at a point on the building several metres above their heads. The object of collective interest was a white sheet, caught in the brickwork and flapping in the wind like a flag at full mast.

'What's going on?' she asked, her voice full of authority. A boy on the edge of the crowd turned to answer her. He stood up noticeably straighter when he saw who was talking.

'Some girl in Nuremburg house had her map blown out of their hands,' he said. Andrea gave him a nod of thanks and walked to the middle of the crowd with Hugo in tow.

A few boys were attempting to get it down by sitting on each other's shoulders, much to the amusement of the gathered crowd.

'Whose map is it?' Andrea asked.

'Lottie's,' Jens said. He was talking to Lottie a few metres away from them, but Hugo hadn't noticed him.

'I can talk for myself, thank you very much,' Lottie said.

'I didn't think you had heard her ask,' Jens said.

'Do you want it back?' Andrea asked. Lottie rolled her eyes.

'Of course I would like it back, but I don't see how anyone without a ladder could reach it,' she said.

'Wait here,' Andrea said nonchalantly. She approached the side of the building with a mountaineer's eye, quickly deciding the fastest way to get to her goal, and her thought was fast enough that there was no hesitation once she had reached the wall. The ledge of a low window, a narrow platform jutting out at an angle from the building, was to be her starting point. Mere seconds after she had taken hold of it, she hand-hauled herself on top of it.

Hugo watched in awe as the pattern repeated itself – Andrea would take hold of a ledge before making a foothold of it; she was always moving, constantly making minor alterations to her position in order to climb more effectively. Imagining himself in her position from the ground, Hugo realised that it was more than a lack of confidence that had stopped him from going up in her place – he could not move as the dark haired girl could. Hugo very much wanted to yell at her to get down, but he was afraid he'd distract her. In the end, he just stood there, heart in mouth.

When only her right hand and foot were left on the ledge, she slowly extended her left arm, reaching out for the map. Andrea felt her palms get sweaty every time the wind picked up a little, and she considered climbing back down several times. She was painfully aware how precariously perched her right foot was, and when she was only a few centimetres away from the map, her foot slipped clean off the ledge.

Andrea's right hand gripped the top of the window she had been skirting as if her life depended on it, and a small corner of her mind reminded her that it did. As soon as the shock wore off, she pushed her foot against the bare wall as if she were abseiling before pulling it back onto the ledge.

There was a cheer on the ground when Andrea regained her footing. As soon as she was secure in her position, she began to move towards the map again. This time, he saw, Andrea was much more careful of her right foot's position. She was still a long time before snatching out at the map, and bringing it close to her. Everyone cheered, but then fell silent again. She still had to get back down.

Andrea was far more cautious coming down. She lowered herself on the ledge, allowing both of her legs to swing until they found the next foothold. Every time she was stable on a level, she stopped for a moment before going down again.

Then there was a relieved applause when she got back onto the ground, and several War School students came up to her to tell her how brave she was.

Andrea thanked them, then came over to Jens, Lottie and Hugo, the last of whom looked as if he had scaled the side of the building rather than just watched someone else do it.

'Here you are,' Andrea said. Hugo could hear that, even though she tried to sound blasé about it, she stuttered on the last word. Lottie accepted the map without a word, and despite the journey it had just taken, it was barely crumpled. Jens laughed at the look on Lottie's face.

'If she wasn't in Hitler house, or a girl, she would be in Victory. She can climb absolutely anything,' Jens said in admiration. Lottie went from being shocked to irate in a matter of seconds.

'Why aren't girls allowed to be in Victory house?' she asked.

'Boys in Victory house are trained to be soldiers,' Jens said. 'We couldn't have a woman in the army. Most Victory house boys become Brandenburgers or join the SS.'

'What are Brandenburgers?' Lottie asked.

'Special forces,' Jens replied. Jens and Lottie walked off together, and Lottie handed Jens the map she had drawn. He examined it, admiring every last detail.

Hugo had remained silent since Andrea came back, and he only spoke again after the bell had gone and they were inside the main block.

'That was the most reckless thing I have ever seen anyone do,' he said quietly.

'I've been climbing things higher and faster for years,' she said, secretly pleased at the worry lines on Hugo's face.

'You almost fell off,' Hugo said.

'That was nothing,' she told him. 'I still had a hand on the ledge,' Hugo stopped walking, and turned to face her.

'Please warn me before you do something like that again,' he said seriously. The intensity of his stare made Andrea blush.

'I will,' she said. Hugo relaxed after that, and in relaxing he realised what he had just said. His face went crimson.

'I mean, you don't have to! It's just that you could get hurt or something...' he started, but quickly trailed off. Andrea shook her head and smiled.

'Come on, or we'll be late,' she said, and Hugo followed her up the stairs towards their next lesson with Karl Ritter.

9

Dinner

'I'm telling you, Andrea, he's just going to beat you at chess again,' Jens said, following Hugo and Andrea up to Hugo's room in the hope of watching Andrea lose to him once more.

'We'll see,' she said. Hugo had a sneaking suspicion she was going to be much harder to beat this time, and he wasn't sure that he wanted to see her squirm again. Jens hadn't even seen him win last time, but he'd been ribbing Andrea about it the whole day regardless.

Hugo pulled his door key from his pocket and opened his room. Jens sighed appreciatively.

'Being a no-bar must be horrible,' he said, 'this room is tiny,'

'Thanks,' Hugo said humourlessly, taking the chessboard out of his suitcase, where he'd replaced it for some reason, instead of putting it away in a drawer.

'Don't worry, you won't be one for long,' Jens said, 'I got here two years ago, when I was thirteen, and I was a two-bar by the time I was fourteen,'

'It took a whole year?' Hugo asked, trying very hard to keep the whine out of his voice.

'It goes faster than you'd think,' Jens said.

'How did you end up a three-bar so quickly?' Hugo asked Jens.

'People leave War School at seventeen, and the majority of them are two and three-bars, so if you end up a two-bar relatively early, there's quite a high chance of you becoming a three-bar at some point,' Jens said.

Hugo took a second to digest this information.

'How are you the four-bar of our house then?' he asked Andrea, who was busying herself with the setting up of the chessboard. 'You can't be much older than I am.'

'Who, me?' Andrea said with a smirk.

'She cheated,' Jens snapped. The look on Andrea's face told Hugo that Jens had brought up an old argument.

'In what way is being invited to join War School early cheating?' she asked, keeping her tone civil.

'You've had a whole three years longer than I have, and two years longer than the rules allow,' Jens said.

'That's not really cheating, more like an advantage,' Andrea said.

'It's a bloody big advantage, you were a two-bar when I got here,' Jens said.

'You've been here for five years?' Hugo asked. Andrea nodded.

'Since I was ten,' she said, 'the first few years were boring; everyone was older than me.'

'Do you go back home every holiday, to see your parents?'

Hugo immediately knew that he had asked a stupid question. Andrea looked away and Jens's eyes widened.

'My parents were killed in a mountaineering accident the year before I came to War School,' Andrea said flatly, working hard to keep her voice level.

'What happened?' Hugo asked. He had spoken impulsively but thought that perhaps she might want him to change the subject. 'It doesn't matter actually, sorry,' he added meekly.

'It's fine,' Andrea said. 'I don't mind talking about it now.' She paused for a moment then went on, 'My parents, my brother and I were climbing the south ridge of Mount Eiger in the Alps in October. It was slightly out of season but it hadn't been a problem until we were about halfway up. I heard a strange sound, something between a bang and a snap, and my mother and my father, who were a good fifty metres above us, started to fall. We would've gone down with them, if not for my mother's quick thinking. As soon as she felt herself falling away, she took the knife from her hip and cut through the cord below her.'

'I'm so sor…' Hugo began.

'Don't be,' she said, cutting off a phrase she had become bored of hearing, 'it happened ages ago and I've still got my brother.'

'Where is he?' Hugo asked, grateful for the change of subject.

'Well, he was serving with the Brandenburgers in Libya about a month ago, now he's in the Carpathian mountains, getting used to the weather before he joins the Third Panzer Army in Russia,' Andrea said.

'He must be a good soldier,' Hugo said.

'One of the very best apparently,' Andrea said wistfully. She allowed herself a moment to reminisce, before clapping her hands together, 'now, why don't I beat you… at chess… a few times before we go down to dinner?'

Four chess games and two hours later, the three of them made their way down the Hitler house staircase. Andrea had been slightly put out the first time she lost, and was almost fuming the second time. She had gone into the third game expecting to lose, and it was the closest one of the four that they had played. Hugo still beat her though.

The fourth game had been between her and Jens, whom she had beaten soundly.

'The thing is,' Jens said, with a finger raised, 'is that I know I'm not good at chess. I told you several times I would lose.'

'After she took your queen,' Hugo pointed out, 'before that you thought you'd beat her,' Jens shrugged and pushed the Hitler house door open.

'You know who you should play?' Andrea said as they walked across the courtyard.

'Who?' Hugo asked.

'Oliver,' she said, 'he's the best chess-player at War School, as well as being a genius.'

'So he says,' Jens said, 'I've yet to see a document that proves he is.'

'According to him, he took a test that gave him a standardised IQ of an hundred and fifty seven,' Andrea said.

'According to him, anyway,' Jens emphasised. A tall boy held the door of the main building open for the three of them, and they made their way to the dining hall.

Hugo was yet to see the dining hall operating at full capacity, and it was truly something impressive. The lights around the edge had been dimmed, but the chandelier shone as brightly as it had at lunch, giving everything in the room below a gold tint. The line serve had been removed, and on every table, in varying stages of being eaten, was a cooked pig, flanked by several roasted chickens and an assortment of vegetables, rice and potatoes.

Hugo tried to avoid looking at the pigs, but the beady slits that made up their eyes seemed to be glaring at him, as if they knew about him what none of the students could. That he was an imposter.

He shook his head to clear the dark thoughts from his head as the three of them chose a table near the door. It was one of only a few tables left, but the food still had steam rising from it.

They were joined almost immediately by Oliver, who, after being described as so amazing looked as distinctively plain as someone in SS uniform can.

'How's your day been?' he asked, sitting to Hugo's right.

'Hugo beat Andrea at chess,' Jens paused for effect, 'four times,' Oliver laughed, and Andrea glared at him.

At that moment, the doors of the dining hall opened and Lottie strode in. Hugo had seen this walk before. She was smug about something. Her eyes darted around the dining hall before they fell on them; and she came to sit down opposite Hugo and next to Jens.

Hugo spotted the source of her smugness immediately. Lottie had two silver bars on her collar, each of them engraved with a little N.

'How did you get those?' Hugo asked. He hadn't had time to start feeling jealous yet, but it was coming.

'I was awarded them this evening,' Lottie said, 'for drawing the map that Andrea rescued.'

'Must've been quite a map,' Hugo said, getting himself some chicken.

'It was,' Jens said, 'I had no idea you could draw so well.'

'She can draw more than well,' Hugo said. Lottie turned to face her brother and smiled. The movement of her head made the bars on her collar glint in the light of the chandelier and the jealousy finally kicked in.

'How is it possible to become a two-bar in a day?' Hugo asked.

'Six hours actually,' she said. Hugo took Andrea's smirk as a personal insult.

'You know what I mean,' Hugo said.

'I'm not sure how they do it in your houses,' she began, addressing the whole table now, 'but in Nuremburg house, someone gets their first bar by proving to a senior figure that they are good enough at drawing to become a cartographer.'

'What do you mean by senior figure?' Hugo asked.

'Either the four bar of my house, the director or any of the teachers,' Lottie said, 'I sort of skipped that step though.'

'How?' Oliver had asked this time. The fact that he had been here for the second longest out of Hugo, Lottie, Andrea, Jens and Oliver, but was the second lowest ranked didn't seem to be sitting very well with him.

'It's usually the first thing you do when arrive at Nuremburg house,' Lottie said, 'they'll sit you down in a room and ask you to draw something for them. I got quite lucky though, this morning they were running a test for the one-bars.'

'But you hadn't been given your first bar yet,' Oliver said.

'I was getting to that. Mr von Ribbentrop vouched for me, he had only just seen my submission,' Lottie explained, 'he assured the woman in charge of the test that I was more than capable of doing whatever it required of me,' Jens, Andrea and Oliver looked surprised.

'He did?' Andrea asked.

'Yeah,' Lottie said. 'Does he do things like that often then?'

'He barely gets involved with the workings of War School, I only see him once a month,' Andrea said.

'You weren't kidding when you said you liked having friends in high places,' Jens said. Lottie laughed.

'That feels like ages ago,' Lottie said.

'You haven't finished,' Oliver interjected, 'how did this test thing make you a two-bar?'

'That's quite simple. It was the test that the one-bars took to see if they were good enough at map drawing to become two-bars,' Lottie said. Oliver nodded and continued to eat, cutting his pork with twice as much force as necessary.

There was silence for a while as they relaxed in each other's company and ate, savouring the gorgeous food in front of them. Between mouthfuls, Jens reopened the conversation.

'So how do you get your third and fourth bars?' he asked Lottie. She finished the last of her chicken and laid her knife and fork down.

'There's an art competition for everyone two-bars and above once every year,' Lottie said. 'The winner gets four and the next five runners-up each get three.'

'When's the next competition?' Jens asked.

'The seventeenth of December,' Lottie said, deep in thought. Hugo could see that she had every intention of entering and winning.

'Ah well. Two-bars in a year is still pretty good going,' Jens said.

'That's true,' Lottie said. Hugo realised that if there wasn't another artist better than her in Nuremburg house, she would be the four bar of the house before the year was out. He groaned inwardly, she was going to be unbearable.

Hugo finished eating a few minutes after the rest of them, and so he was put in charge of returning their plates.

Where the line serve had been at lunch, a cart laden with sponge cakes now stood. On the top of the cart was a sign, informing the students that taking more than one cake for your table was an offence punishable by detention. Hugo took one and carried it back to his table.

He arrived just in time to see a smartly-dressed man piling the remnants of their dinner onto a different cart. Oliver, who had spearheaded the effort to get Hugo to take the plates, gave an apologetic smile.

'It turns out you didn't need to take them after all,' he said, 'is that sponge?' he asked, getting up out of his seat and relieving Hugo of the cake.

'What are you all doing this evening?' Oliver asked, tucking into his cake. There was an assortment of shrugs and mumbles around the table. Hugo himself was only half listening; the sponge was currently his primary focus.

'What did you have in mind?' Hugo asked as he reached over to cut himself a second slice.

'Is the grand piano still in Hitler house?' Oliver asked, looking at Jens, who sighed.

'They're hardly going to move a piano are they?' he said. 'But I'm not finished yet,' he added.

'You told me you'd be finished within a day this time last week,' Oliver said.

'I remember you saying that,' Andrea said. Jens scowled at her.

'All right, fine. I finished last Tuesday,' Jens said.

'At last,' Oliver said, with a smile, 'Why has it taken so long?'

'Well,' Jens began, shuffling in his seat a little, 'I haven't just been learning it; it's not really a piano piece, so I've had to transcribe the music.'

'What does that mean?' Hugo asked.

'It means that before I could start learning it, I had to adapt the notes to be played on a piano,' Jens explained.

'That must be so difficult,' said Hugo.

Jens shrugged, with genuine modesty, Hugo thought. 'It just takes practice, that's all,' Jen said.

'So when are you going to play us the piece?' Oliver asked.

'Now, if you're up for it,' Jens replied. The other four nodded, quickly finished their cake at the table and left the dining hall.

10

Jens the Pianist

'Jens, what on earth is the difference between this one and the last three?' Andrea asked irritably. Jens had been leading Andrea, Hugo, Lottie and Oliver around the building, which was far larger than Hugo's brief tour with Oliver had suggested, in search of a music room with the right piano, 'what was wrong with the first piano we saw?' she added.

Jens made an odd face, as if someone had suggested he sleep in a bog.

'I didn't like that one,' he said shortly. Andrea groaned.

If War School had one shortfall, it was that the rooms were not arranged in any logical order - another reminder of the building's past life as a country house. The music rooms were dotted in and around the classrooms and the lecture halls, and although Jens had dragged his friends in and out of four of them, he seemed to at least know where he was going.

A few piano-free minutes went by before they hit on a room that had a large window and a brown grand in a corner.

'Lovely, a Beckstein!' Jens exclaimed. He walked over to the window and opened the curtains before sitting down on the piano stool.

They each picked a seat in the room and moved it towards Jens, making a crescent. Without any announcement, Jens started to play.

The first thing Hugo felt was disappointment. The song had no regular pattern and stopped whenever Jens felt like it. Calling this mess a melody was a stretch.

'What on earth are you doing?' Oliver asked. Jens stopped immediately.

'Oh!' he laughed to himself, 'I was warming up my hands. I want to play it perfectly.' Hugo was relieved.

They sat in silence, waiting for him to begin. Lottie, who was sitting furthest to the left, was the only one who could see Jens's hands as they warmed up, and Hugo saw a look of amazement flash across his sister's eyes.

Hugo and Lottie's mother Anna had been able to play the piano, usually the upright in their living room at home, but comparing her mother's playing to Jens's was like comparing the flight of a paper aeroplane to that of an eagle.

Jens stopped as abruptly as he had started, 'All right,' he said half to himself. He sat up bolt upright and cracked his knuckles.

If you had asked any of them afterwards, they wouldn't be able to tell you when he had started playing. There didn't seem to have been a first note, the same way there never seems to be a first raindrop.

Oliver was the only one of them who had any experience with music, and he gasped when he heard what Jens was playing. He didn't hear himself gasp though; the music had already enveloped him.

Jens's hands were fantastically fast, but he was in complete control of them. He never seemed rushed and never pressed a note harder or softer than it needed to be. The music was in two distinct parts, but trying to explain it as any more than that was like digging in quicksand, the second you formed a coherent thought about it, the music would sweep that idea away.

What made Jens's playing so amazing was the fact that the two parts were pieces in their own right. Jens's right hand bounced up and down the piano so quickly that one key would have barely come back up before the next had been pressed. His left hand was slower at times, like a march, but at other times it would be faster than the right. The easiest way to imagine it would be a typewriter being used by a dozen different people, each pressing a letter a fraction of a second after the next.

All of a sudden, the music slowed. It didn't feel like it was ending though, it felt like it was reaching the climax.

For a few seconds, none of the keys were being pressed and there was silence, but the air sparked with suspense.

Then the song came back, one hand almost as quickly as before and the other much slower, but both of them were far quieter.

The easiest way to describe the next thing that happened would be an explosion. Not a normal explosion, though, because a normal explosion is impossible to tame. This one was only as wild as Jens willed it to be. It was very close to banging, but to use a word as crude as banging to describe Jens's playing would be a crime.

He took a breath before he began what was recognisably the finale. For the first time, his face started to go red with the strain of what he was doing. Both hands were going faster than they had at any point before, and together they would get softer then harder then softer again, all the while never changing pace.

The music slowed one final time, and with a flourish and a last chord, it was over.

Jens's hands, which had been so dazzling and accurate a second earlier, slumped to his side. His audience, which was in a state of shock similar to that of a new-born baby, were completely silent. Each of them wanted with every fibre of their being to clap, to applaud and praise his playing as much as they could, but it was all they could do to sit there, mouths agape.

'What did you think?' he asked, turning on his stool. He had to wait at least half a minute for an answer.

'Perfect,' Lottie said. Hugo saw Jens go a deep shade of crimson when he saw how seriously Lottie had said it.

'How on earth...' Oliver started, 'that was La Follia wasn't it?' Jens nodded with a smile like a naughty schoolboy.

'I did say I had to transpose,' he said.

'I assumed you were transposing a piece for one instrument!' Oliver said, aghast. Jens turned to face Hugo and Andrea, who were sat to Oliver's right.

'Why are you here?' Andrea asked. Jens looked confused.

'What do you mean?' he asked.

'I know what she's saying,' Hugo began, 'you could be touring around the world, playing for kings and presidents.'

Jens laughed. 'Pianists are in unsurprisingly low demand at the moment, what with the war on.' Jens looked wistfully out into the window before he continued; 'I would love to play at the Berghof though, in front of the Führer and my uncle. That would be the greatest honour imaginable!'

Reality hit Hugo like a brick; it presented itself in Jens's words and scared him to the point that he considered leaving the room.

He knew that two of the people sitting mere feet away from him, one of whom he'd started to nurture feelings for, would hate him if they knew what he was. For them, going to Adolf Hitler's private residence and playing the piano for him and Joseph Goebbels was a dream rather than a nightmare.

'I'm sure if you showed your uncle what you just showed us, he would take you there in a heartbeat,' Oliver said.

'Oh, I'm sure my uncle is too busy with his work in the Nazi party to bother with my piano playing,' Jens said.

One by one, they all grudgingly got to their feet. Jens flicked off the lights in the room and closed the door behind them.

It took them no time at all to get to the courtyard, and they parted ways as soon as they reached the fountain.

The warmth and light of Hitler house was like a hug after the cold, dark courtyard. The dull thud of three sets of feet on the stairs broke the silence of the building, and they hurried up, as not to disturb it more than was necessary. Hugo turned off on the first floor and was initially surprised to have no one at his side.

He turned back and saw Jens and Andrea going up the next set, and he remembered that as senior members of the house, they slept in larger rooms on the floor above.

'Oh, Hugo?' Jens said, stopping his ascent.

'Yeah?' Hugo asked.

'You were wondering why I wasn't out somewhere being a pianist, right?'

Hugo nodded.

'I got a scholarship to some music school in Dresden,' added Jens, 'at about the same time that my uncle suggested to my parents that I come here.'

'Why didn't you go?' Hugo asked.

'I really don't know,' Jens said. I couldn't see myself playing music for my whole life, and there was something about War School that drew me towards this place. I had a sense… yes, a sense somehow… that something very important was waiting for me here.' He gave a shrug. 'Perhaps I've found it.' He nodded to Hugo and made his way up to the second floor.

It only occurred to Hugo when he was lying in bed that Jens could well have been talking about Lottie.

11

Hugo and Frederick

The rest of the week Hugo worked hard, saw his new friends and tried to reconcile the different ideas he had of Jens; the confident three-bar, the brilliant pianist, and the nephew of the twisted Nazi.

While Hugo was slowly beginning to feel a little less like he had a Star of David tattooed on his cheek, he did occasionally feel a panic when he saw the size of some of the boys in Victory house. He knew they'd break his neck with their bare hands if they found out his secret.

This was a fact that had either escaped his sister or evidently failed to worry her. Hugo had asked her about it on the Thursday of their first week, cornering her outside Nuremburg house and speaking in a hushed tone.

'How do you deal with it?' he had asked.

'I don't think about it,' Lottie had said. 'Whether I worry or not, I can't change the fact that we're Jews, or that our dad sacrificed his life to try to keep that a secret, and very likely succeeded. You're just causing yourself unnecessary stress.' She had left without another word, walking up to the main building with Jens.

Today was Friday, and Hugo found himself making his way through the main building towards his lesson, flanked by Jens and Andrea.

'What do you reckon we'll be doing today?' Hugo asked Andrea as they made their way through the main block.

'Who knows,' Andrea said, 'though if it's ranked games I'm sitting as far away from you as possible,' she added.

Hugo laughed. 'If it is, I think I might just give Frederick a game,' Hugo mused.

'Talk of the devil,' Jens said, motioning his head towards Frederick, who had appeared out of thin air and was striding towards their classroom, 'where did you come from?' Jens asked him.

'Breakfast,' he replied shortly.

'Not what I meant,' Jens said, 'you weren't walking behind us a second ago.'

'Whatever,' Frederick said, walking off. A glance to his right, at a door off the corridor that had been left ajar, clicked the pieces together in Jens's head.

'We're not allowed to use the lounge rooms to get to lessons,' Jens said, in an uncanny imitation of Fredrick's words from a few days before.

'I don't answer to you anyway,' Fredrick said, slightly uneasily, 'we're of equal rank, you can't tell me what to do'.

'No, you answer to Andrea,' Jens said. He turned around to look at Andrea, who, along with Hugo, had slowed her walk to leave Jens and Frederick to argue alone. Jens looked pointedly at her until she spoke.

'What?' she asked.

'Haven't you been listening?' Jens asked.

'Why would we have been?' she asked, 'I don't care about your feud with him, and neither does Hugo. Right?'

'Um,' Hugo said, trying to think of an answer that wouldn't offend either of them.

'Ugh, you're completely spineless,' Andrea said to Hugo before returning to Jens, 'deal with him yourself. Don't drag me into it.'

'What are you going to do now that you've lost your attack dog?' Frederick said to Jens, 'you haven't got anything over me.'

'I don't appreciate being called an attack dog,' Andrea said icily, cutting across Jens reply, 'if you've got any brains at all you'll apologise for that remark and make your merry way to our lesson.'

'I don't appreciate Jens trying to get me into trouble for something he does pretty much every morning,' Frederick retorted.

'Listen you whelp,' Andrea said. 'I couldn't give half a damn about your argument, but if you ever call me an attack dog again, I'll have you expelled faster than you can beg to stay.' Andrea didn't shout, but Hugo felt that her saying this levelly and calmly made her even scarier.

'Andrea, what you've just said is complete nonsense,' Frederick told her.

'Is it? Give me ten minutes and I could have a letter on the director's desk saying that I caught you smoking and recommending that you are booted out,' Andrea said calmly.

'That's a lie. I'll deny it,' Frederick said, his confidence beginning to wane.

'So? I'll have two witnesses,' Andrea said, pointing to Hugo and Jens.

'You wouldn't,' Frederick said.

'Try me,' Andrea replied simply. It took about four seconds for Frederick to cave in.

'Sorry,' he said, tail between his legs, 'it won't happen again.'

'It had better not,' Andrea said, and with that, she strode towards their lesson with the three boys in tow.

There was a small crowd outside their classroom door, and as they approached, a few of the crowd looked at Hugo.

'What's going on?' Andrea asked the assembled students, 'where's Mr Ritter?'

'He hasn't arrived. The new boy, Hugo, is one of the captains for the war game this afternoon, and so everyone's waiting to see what instructions he gives.' It was Michael Bauer, the three-bar who had sat behind Hugo during his first lesson. 'By the way, I've heard you've got a thing for him, that new boy, I mean?'

'I don't have a thing for him!' Andrea said indignantly. Michael shrugged.

'I didn't say what that thing was, but there's certainly something there,' he said. Hugo coughed quite loudly and cut in.

'What was that about captains?' he asked.

'Oh, I didn't see you there, Hugo,' Michael said, a little embarrassed, 'right, well someone from Hitler house takes control of each group of boys from Victory house whenever they have a war game. So as well as it being a contest between the two groups, it's a contest between the two captains.'

'And I'm against Frederick?' Hugo asked.

'Correct. They always put you up against someone ranked highly for your first one, to see what you're made of,' Michael said.

'I bet you're glad you didn't get him,' Jens said with a smirk to Andrea, 'he might have beaten you again.'

'Shut up,' she said.

'What was that?' Michael asked.

'Doesn't matter,' Andrea said quickly, 'what's the scenario?'

'I think he's defending a bunker in the woods,' Michael said.

'Yes he is,' it was Frederick. An opportunity to regain the face he had lost earlier had presented itself, and he was grinning from ear to ear, 'and I'm going to make you squeal,' he said happily, 'I've never lost an attack on the bunker and that won't change today.'

'Go darken someone else's day, Frederick,' Jens said.

'I'm supposed to be outside Victory house in ten minutes, I don't have time to talk to you,' Frederick said curtly.

'Go on then,' Jens said.

'I will,' Frederick replied, already walking away.

'Don't I have to come as well?' Hugo asked. Frederick sighed and stopped walking.

'Follow me then,' he said.

Hugo stood in front of ten of the largest boys he'd ever seen in his life. The shortest of them was half a head taller than he was, and though the room was easily large enough to fit twenty, Hugo felt more claustrophobic with each passing second. He almost missed Frederick, who'd left him outside the building without as much as a good-bye. Frederick, too, seemed to have assumed that there was something going on between him and Andrea, and had grilled him about her the whole way.

He couldn't pretend that he hadn't thought about her like that; it would've been almost impossible not to, what with all the time that they had been spending together. She was lovely to be around, and she was just so beautiful...

A massive paw of a hand pushed Hugo in the chest and he went toppling backwards into the wall behind him: One of the assembled boys had grown tired of waiting and decided to wake Hugo from his torpor.

'What was that for?' Hugo asked, careful not to sound irritated. The boy who'd pushed him brought his feet together and spoke in a flat, army tone.

'To check you were awake, sir, your eyes had glazed over,' he said. There was something untoward in the way he spoke, but Hugo couldn't put his finger on it.

'My eyes were open, how could I have fallen asleep?' Hugo asked.

'I've seen it happen before sir,' he said. There it was, Hugo realised, the boy was saying 'sir' with as much derision as he could muster.

'Right. Well, um... Do any of you have any idea what we're doing?' Hugo said.

'Sure,' the boy said, 'we're going to get absolutely destroyed by Frederick.'

'Right' Hugo said, 'but how exactly do we stop him from doing that?' The boy laughed.

'We don't, but these are our tools in failure,' he said, striding over to a metal cabinet and producing a black rifle.

'I know, paint-filled pellets fired out of guns,' Hugo said, 'if one hits you you're "dead" I assume?'

'Indeed,' the boy said with a smirk. He lined the rifle up at Hugo and shot at him, the pellet bursting a foot above his head and spraying pink flecks into his hair. Hugo was so surprised that he didn't move to avoid it, and his resulting disorientation produced the expected reaction in the huge boys. The laughter had not stopped even after Hugo had got to his feet.

'Fredrick hasn't lost in three years of attacking the bunker. We haven't got a hope,' the boy that had shot at Hugo said through a mocking smile.

'First time for everything,' Hugo said.

'Not necessarily. He could keep that record until he leaves War School,' the boy said, his mirth transitioning to back to irritation.

'That's no reason not to try!' Hugo said desperately, 'if there's a map or something, we could lay it out and plan what we're going to do.'

'Who's going to lead then?' he asked, 'you? No chance. I'm not taking orders from some dewy-eyed child that probably doesn't even shave yet.'

'You have to listen to me,' Hugo said. 'I've been appointed commander of our force, and I'm from Hitler House.'

'Officially, yes, you're in charge,' the boy replied, 'but I'm not too sure how you're going to enforce your decisions,' he stood up straighter and crossed his massive arms to emphasise this point.

'I'll...'

'Morning boys!'

Hugo had never been more relieved to hear that voice in his life. As soon as Andrea made her presence known, the group of boys stood up straight and all gazed at her in varying degrees of adoration. 'Morning Jürgen,' she said, addressing the boy who had been goading Hugo.

'Morning Andrea,' Jürgen replied. He was a different person now: There was a genuine smile on his face and his tone smacked of deference.

'Oh, Hugo!' Andrea exclaimed. 'I didn't expect to find you here! How are you finding it?' Hugo's look of relief surely answered her question for him.

'It's great,' Hugo said sarcastically. Then he had an idea, 'We were just about to get a map out weren't we?' He looked straight at Jürgen, who'd shot him daggers the second Andrea couldn't see his face.

'Yes we were,' Jürgen said. 'Lads, get the map and a table out sharpish,' the Victory house boys moved with a frightening efficiency: the table and map were located and set up within a minute. One or two of them made a big show of lifting the table, and they all seemed to be throwing out their chests and flexing their arms as much as they reasonably could. Andrea looked at Hugo and rolled her eyes.

The ten of them stood to attention behind the table in a line, awaiting further orders. They were all making a conscious effort not to stare at Andrea, and in doing so made it extremely obvious that they were. Hugo took pride in the fact that he would have liked her just as much even if she wasn't as attractive as she was, but it certainly didn't hurt that she looked as good as she did.

'I hope you're all going to do what Hugo tells you to do,' Andrea said to the assembled boys, 'he might be new here, but I know he'll be as good as anyone in Hitler house at leading you all.'

'Certainly, Miss,' Jürgen said.

'Excellent, I'm glad you agree,' Andrea replied, she nodded to Hugo and headed away.

Jürgen spoke as soon as he guessed she was out of earshot.

'We're still not listening to you,' he said. Hugo sighed.

As if on cue, Andrea turned swiftly around and headed back towards them. Hugo was expecting her to address the room of boys again, perhaps to say something she'd forgotten, and so he was incredibly surprised when Andrea stopped walking a foot away from his face and kissed him on the lips.

It wasn't a peck on the cheek; it was a proper kiss of a sort he'd never had before. It wasn't over quickly either; it must have lasted for half a minute, or even longer.

Hugo felt he was going to explode with happiness. The feeling of her mouth against his and the fragrance of her hair and the softness of her cheeks against his made him feel that, for a moment, he was in a small and breathtakingly amazing world of his own.

As Andrea finally broke the kiss and moved away from him, Hugo gasped and realised that he was so excited that he had been holding his breath for the entire duration of the kiss. When he opened his eyes, Andrea was still inches away and smiling radiantly.

'You'd better beat Frederick,' she said softly.

'Yeah… I'll do my best,' Hugo muttered, still stunned, still not believing what had just happened. She laughed at the confused look on his face, and her laugh prompted a smile in Hugo – her laughter was the sweetest sound he'd ever heard.

For the first time since she'd come back in, she looked at the rest of the boys in the room, all of whom were now staring at Hugo.

'Good luck to you all,' she said, and with that, she turned on her toes and left the room, closing the door behind her.

The boys in front of Hugo stared at him with a mix of jealousy and reverence, but underlying those two emotions was a great deal of awe – Hugo didn't think it would be too hard to get them to listen to him anymore.

'Can we get on with planning now?' he asked them all. There was a pause.

'All right sir,' Jürgen said. The derision was gone and he spoke with what Hugo thought was a resentful admiration. 'We're going to get smashed regardless.'

'Perhaps not,' Hugo said, looking down at the complex tunnels of the bunker on the map in front of him, 'what do people usually do when defending the bunker?' Jürgen thought for a moment.

'Well it's meant to be fairly easy to defend,' he said, 'The entrance to the bunker is a shed of corrugated iron, in the middle of a clearing. The tunnels beneath it spread out several hundred feet in different directions, and one route amongst those tunnels leads to a main room.'

'So it's like a maze?' Hugo asked. Jürgen nodded.

'The problem is that Fredrick knows the whole thing back-wards. He knows all the routes and hiding places. There's no ambushing him down there.' The boy said. Hugo began to smile, wondering where the idea beginning to form in his head had come from. The word ambushed flicked a switch in Hugo's brain.

'I've got a plan' he said. He lay his palms flat on the table and began to explain his plot to defeat Fredrick.

**

Frederick loved the beginning of a mock battle, especially when he was up against a no bar. The new students in Hitler house were usually clueless, and it was incredibly easy to figure out what they would do in any given situation.

A klaxon signalling the start of the battle went off in the distance, and Frederick's small army of ten made its way towards the bunker. He barely needed to give this lot orders anymore, they had served under him dozens of times and knew exactly what he wanted them to do.

The clearing the bunker was in sat deep inside the wood that surrounded War School, and so even though it was midday, the visibility of Frederick's troops was extremely impaired. He wasn't worried about an ambush though, Hugo and his boys had to be within a hundred metres of the Bunker or they lost the game automatically.

Suddenly, Frederick's troops stopped walking, and the highest ranked of them turned to look at Frederick.

'He's put two guards outside the bunker doors. I could hit them from here if you'd like,' Frederick shook his head.

'No point alerting everyone inside to our presence,' he said. 'I have an idea. You lot all hate being under the command of no bars, right?'

'Clueless idiots,' the boy agreed.

'Right. So how about we surround them and ask the two guards to let us in and avoid being shot?' Frederick asked.

'Worth a go,' the boy said, 'and if it doesn't work, we can just shoot them.'

'Exactly,' Frederick said, 'let's do it then.'

Frederick didn't need to give them specific commands; they knew exactly what he wanted.

The boy he'd been talking to nodded towards the bunker and the ten boys moved with almost superhuman speed.

One of the guards was about to fire at them, but he quickly decided against it when he realised they were outnumbered eleven to two.

Frederick sauntered towards the guards, enjoying the feeling of power he gained from the helplessness of the two of them.

'Drop your guns,' he ordered. Both guards followed Frederick's command immediately, holding their hands in the air. ' I don't want to shoot you, and you don't want to be shot, so step aside, let me in and everyone can end today without any bruises.'

'You make a compelling argument,' one of the guards said, 'but it's been locked.'

'Who has the key?' Frederick asked.

'I do,' the same guard replied.

'Hand it over then,' Frederick said, holding out his palm.

'Oh sure, one second,' the guard reached into his pocket and dug around for a little, before removing his hand and giving Frederick a middle finger.

'Fine,' Frederick said, his cheeks going a little red, 'shoot them.'

Frederick's troops obliged. The rules were that, once someone had been shot once, they were dead and couldn't be shot nor could they shoot again, but these rules were rarely enforced, if ever. Both guards took at least five of the paint pellets each. To their credit, neither of them screamed or shouted, but they were out of the game, Hugo only had eight men left.

Frederick stepped over to the boy that had sworn at him and put his hand into the boy's pocket, 'if you resist I'll have them shoot you again,' Frederick found the key in the boy's back pocket. He dangled it in front of the guard's face before opening the Bunker door. 'I was going to get it off you anyway. Could have saved yourself the discomfort,' Frederick said.

'Made a hell of a lot more noise this way,' the guard said. His companion elbowed him in the ribs and glared at him.

'What was that?' Frederick asked, one foot through the doorway.

'Nothing,' he said. Frederick couldn't see what Hugo might do to outwit him, so he let it slide and continued into the Bunker.

The underground structure could be daunting to someone that was new to it, but Frederick knew the twists and turns of the bunker like the back of his hand.

He and his men went through the bunker methodically, taking care to make sure that every room was empty.

Occasionally, a no-bar would keep all his men as one group and stay inside the main room of the bunker. This was a frustrating thing for Frederick, but he was fairly sure his men could overpower Hugo's. Especially now that it was eleven on nine.

As they approached the main room, Frederick began to plan the report that he was going to give. Hugo hadn't shown any tactical nous at all, and had guaranteed that he would be outnumbered in the final skirmish by leaving two guards outside the bunker. If he chose his words correctly, he could get Hugo kicked out for incompetence. That would show Andrea.

'Ready when you are, Fred,' it was Kellan, a thuggish boy in Frederick's group who was scary even by Victory house standards.

'Open it up,' Frederick said calmly.

It was empty.

There wasn't a soul inside the main room, and for the first time during the war game, Frederick was unsure of himself. This had never happened before.

'Where are they?' he asked the empty room.

His men, edging in from behind him, were just as bewildered as he was, and none of them had the slightest idea what to do.

About fifty metres away from Frederick and his men, eleven teenagers crouched down low at the entrance to the bunker.

'We could just lock them in,' one of the guards suggested, 'let them starve.'

'Wow,' Hugo said, 'isn't that murder?' the guard shrugged.

'Frederick wouldn't be missed,' he said. A few of the guards nodded in agreement, and Hugo realised that they were actually considering it!

'We are not killing them,' Hugo said to the boys. 'It isn't just Frederick down there remember? Surely at least one of you has a friend in there with him?'

'I suppose you're right,' the guard said, 'but I'm coming down. I want to be a part of the shootout.'

'No you aren't,' Hugo said, surprised at the authority in his voice. 'I want to beat him fairly. If we cheat he'll have an excuse to not accept defeat.' The guard looked like he was going to protest but decided against it, seeing the sense in what Hugo said.

'My my Hugo, it looks like you've grown a pair,' Jürgen said, 'shouldn't we be making our way down?'

'Not yet. Let's wait a little,' Hugo said.

'Isn't that a little risky? What if they come back up?' Jürgen asked.

'Then we'll shoot the hell out of them here, but it's a calculated risk anyway. Frederick has no respect for me at all, so he won't have them on high alert,' Hugo said.

'That doesn't make much sense,' Jürgen said honestly. Hugo thought about it.

'I don't suppose it does,' he said, 'go on then. Let's do it.'

Nine of the eleven boys made their way down towards the main room of the Bunker. They were not as careful as Frederick - they only took a quick look inside the rooms that they went past - but they were far quieter.

Hugo was pleased to see that the main room's door had been left wide open, and a peek around the corner told him that Frederick's men were milling about doing nothing.

'Perfect,' Hugo said.

'Let's go!' Jürgen whispered emphatically.

'No wait,' Hugo said quietly, 'no one is to shoot Frederick. He's mine.'

The Victory house boys nodded excitedly. This adrenaline rush was what they lived for.

'Three, Two, One... Go!' Hugo yelled the final command; he didn't see much wrong with shouting just before the racket that the guns would create.

The boys rushed into the room and fired several shots around at random, before committing what would be described as a massacre if the bullets were lead rather than paint.

They were extremely good at what they did, and the confusion amongst Frederick's men helped immensely - only three of them were still without paint on their uniforms by the time they had their guns. By this point, Frederick had realised that he wasn't being shot at deliberately.

'Come on then,' Frederick said. The anger on his face was slightly diluted by the shock and surprise that he felt, and after his last soldier had been shot, he stood in the middle of the room with his hands behind his back, 'shoot me then,' he said.

'If you don't mind, Jürgen,' Hugo said, extending his hand to receive Jürgen's gun. The boy handed it to him in one hand and Hugo took it with both, struggling at first to hold it up.

He took aim at Frederick, and after the sight had steadied itself on his chest, he pulled the trigger.

Or rather he decided to pull the trigger. His finger wouldn't oblige.

There was something about training a gun on a live target that didn't sit well with Hugo - even if it was a person he disliked as much as Frederick.

'Oh dear,' Jürgen said, patronising Hugo a little, 'I'll do it if you can't stomach it.

This goaded Hugo into action. He took aim at Frederick and shot him.

Hugo's men whooped and cheered as soon as the paint bullet marked Frederick's chest, and Jürgen began a crescendo of applause that reverberated around the bunker.

'That was very well done,' Frederick said, surprisingly genuine. 'The best I've ever seen a no bar do.'

'Thanks,' Hugo said with a smile. Hugo's smile was a little forced, because now there was no planning or shooting going on, Hugo was reminded of what the eight massive boys in front of him would do if they found out who and what he was. The thought made him shudder, and as they carried him out of the bunker and towards Hitler house, in triumph, his expression became darker and darker. He knew he would never be comfortable here at War School.

12

Dr Goebbels

Hugo spent a great deal of the first month at War School in Andrea's company. The bar he had earned against Frederick in the war game had stopped him from feeling like a novice in her shadow, and whilst he was a long way from the lofty heights of Andrea's four bars, his first had filled him with confidence.

Andrea heard at the end of the second week that her brother had joined the Third Panzer Army. Her mood deteriorated from that day onwards. She was obviously extremely worried about her brother, and she would press him for information whenever she wrote. Unfortunately, all letters from the front went through a myriad of censorship that left them distinctly lacking in detail.

Even though Hugo was in Andrea's company, she hadn't kissed him again or, in fact, even very explicitly acknowledged that she had that one time. She would change the subject immediately when it looked like Hugo might bring it up, and when they weren't talking about the war or her brother, she was extremely standoffish with him. He had no idea what to do.

Oliver took up the majority of the time that Hugo spent outside of lessons and away from Andrea. The curly-haired boy was relieved he'd found another likeminded soul at War School – it was as if he had been waiting for a friend like

Hugo, who understood a little bit more about what was happening in the country, to talk to. Hugo became his outlet, and Oliver spent the next month telling Hugo exactly what he thought of what was going on.

'I don't think it's right to blame everyone in Germany for the Nazis though,' Oliver had said once. He usually chose one of the lounge rooms in the main building to talk, obviously not wanting to be overheard.

'What do you mean?' Hugo asked. The way he had grown up, it had been very easy to see every German as an enemy. 'Anyone who doesn't do anything about them is just as guilty.' Oliver was very surprised to hear that from Hugo.

'That's hardly fair. You're asking people to choose between being martyrs or Nazis,' Oliver said. 'I think Hitler's to blame. It all comes back to him doesn't it? He's completely cracked.' He stopped talking at that point. That was the first time Hugo had heard anyone but his mother badmouth the Führer and he reeled a little from it. They were both all too aware that, if anyone had overheard what Oliver had just said, he - Oliver - would be shot. Possibly Hugo too, as a conspirator. They were more careful after that.

'SAFIN!' Ritter yelled Hugo's surname from across the lecture hall and roused him from his stupor.

'Yes sir?' Hugo was sunk if he asked him anything about the lesson; he hadn't been paying the slightest bit of attention.

'What did I just say?' he asked, folding his arms. Hugo considered the little boy's trick of repeating his question, but one look at the man's expression killed that idea. He was not in the mood.

He glanced over at Andrea, who was sitting to his right. She shrugged and grinned.

'I wasn't listening either,' she whispered.

'Well?' Ritter asked.

'I wasn't listening sir,' Hugo said quietly.

'Speak up!' he yelled. This was the first altercation Hugo had had with Ritter in his first month at War School, and Hugo prayed that it would be his last.

'I wasn't listening, sir,' Hugo said again.

'As I thought,' Ritter said, triumphantly, 'after lessons today...' the man never got to finish dictating Hugo's punishment because he was interrupted by the opening of the door.

It wasn't a cautious opening, as you'd expect from someone interrupting a lesson, the new arrival practically threw the door open.

Ritter looked set to chastise the person rude enough to interrupt one of his lessons, but the moment he saw who it was, the reprimand turned on his tongue and dived back down his throat.

The face was instantly familiar for it had been the source of countless nightmares for Hugo. But now, the narrow chin and pointed, almost elflike features of the man's face held a new familiarity – hints of them could be seen on Jens' face. There were obvious differences; where Jens had blue eyes and blond hair, the man had black pupils and hair to match. Features that sharpened the man's face made Jens' strong, but the similarity was such that there could be no doubt.

This was Joseph Goebbels.

'Good evening,' Goebbels said. He looked at their teacher and raised a narrow eyebrow.

'Ah, of course, Ritter,' he said hurriedly, 'students, allow me to introduce Dr Joseph Goebbels, the uncle of our very own Jens Goebbels and the Minister for Public Enlightenment in the German Reich.'

There was a crescendo of applause, with some of the students standing up and whooping. After he had had his fill, Dr Goebbels waved a hand to silence them.

'Three of you are to carry out a vitally important mission that comes straight from the Führer's desk. These three...' Dr Goebbels paused for effect. He surveyed the hall. Every single student had their hand up, '...have already been chosen,' there was a collective sigh, and all of the raised arms dropped, 'these three students are my nephew, Jens; Andrea Ducasse and Hugo Safin,' Hugo felt as confused as everyone around him looked.

The three of them made their way to the front, and stood at Goebbels' side.

'Excuse me,' it was Frederick. He was sitting at the front, a metre or so away from Hugo, radiating jealousy.

'Yes?' Dr Goebbels asked. Frederick opened his mouth and then closed it. He needed to pick his words carefully.

'Andrea is the highest ranked person here, and Jens is second,' Frederick said. Goebbels looked blankly at him.

'Why are you stating the obvious?' he asked sharply. There was no way Frederick was going to lead Goebbels into saying something.

'Well, why is Hugo going rather than me?' Frederick asked, 'I'm third highest ranked after all,' he added.

'I understood that,' Dr Goebbels said.

'So why is he?' Frederick asked. He seemed to be under the impression that he had gotten through to the man.

'Because I want him,' Goebbels said simply.

'But why?' Frederick asked. Goebbels raised an eyebrow.

'Are you saying that I have made a mistake in picking Mr Safin over you?' Goebbels challenged.

'Yes I am,' Frederick said. Goebbels seemed surprised that he'd had the guts to say it, and he scratched his chin as if thinking.

'On what grounds?' Goebbels asked. Frederick got out of his chair and walked up to Dr Goebbels.

Although he had a good few inches over him, there was no question as to where the power was. What had been a brave gesture in Frederick's mind now felt foolhardy, but there was no going back now.

'Anything that he...' Frederick almost spat the words at Hugo, 'can do, I can do better,' Dr Goebbels stopped scratching his chin and smiled at Frederick.

'Really?' he said, in manner that almost suggested interest, 'and you're sure about that are you?' Frederick nodded confidently.

'I am,' he said.

'Pochemu ty tak glup?' Dr Goebbels asked quickly. Hugo chuckled.

'Pardon?' Frederick asked. Goebbels repeated the words, 'What does that mean?' Frederick asked weakly. Goebbels shook his head, the same way a disappointed teacher would.

'What a shame. If you were half as clever as you were arrogant then perhaps you would have some idea,' Goebbels said. He turned to Hugo, 'Pochemu on tak glupo?' Hugo thought for a second.

'Mozhet byt, on upal pri rozhdenii. Ya ne znayu,' Hugo said with a shrug. Goebbels laughed heartily and clapped Hugo on the back. Never before had he felt such an odd mix of pride and disgust. He could tell by the odd mixture of raised eyebrows and frowns the others were dying to know what had been said. He would tell them later. They would enjoy the joke.

'That is why he is coming and not you,' Goebbels said. With that, he led the three of them out of the hall. Goebbels walked them quickly to the director's office, where he beckoned them to sit down.

'I would like you to stay here and wait for me to fetch two more students,' Goebbels said.

Who else is coming, Uncle?' Jens asked.

'Hugo, you have a sister I believe?' Hugo nodded, 'is her Russian as good as yours?' he asked. Hugo nodded again.

'Better even,' he said.

'Then she will come as well,' Goebbels said. Hugo could have sworn that Jens's eyes glinted at the mention of his sister. 'The Führer has instructed me to get a student from Fatherland house,' he scowled. 'I doubt any of those swots will want to come, but orders are orders.' Goebbels walked off and, as he did, Hugo noticed the man had a slight limp. Goebbels was in enough control to hide it, but it was definitely there.

'What did he say?' Jens asked as soon as the door had closed, 'in Russian I mean,'

'He asked why Frederick was so stupid,' Hugo said, 'and I said it could be because he was dropped at birth.' Jens laughed and Andrea smiled a little but, the second she saw Hugo look over, she turned away.

'What is it?' Hugo asked her, 'you haven't said anything since we were in the lesson.' She'd obviously been waiting for Hugo to say something of the sort, because she replied immediately.

'When were you planning to tell me you were Russian?' she asked acidly. Now he understood.

'Half Russian, and it just didn't come up. I would have told you if you'd asked,' Hugo said, perhaps a shade dishonestly. 'Why does it even matter?'

'Why does it matter?' Andrea repeated, raising her voice slightly. 'My brother is fighting the Russians at the moment! One of your relatives might end up being the one that kills him.'

'My mother was an only child, and we haven't heard from my grandparents on her side since the purges started,' Hugo said. He didn't know quite how he should feel about that, he'd never even met them.

'How on earth did your mother come to live in Germany?' Jens asked, trying to steer the conversation in a more positive direction.

'She met my father when he was on a business trip to the Soviet Union,' said Hugo. 'He used to sell typewriters for my grandfather's company.'

'Used to?' Jens asked. 'What does he do now?' Hugo didn't reply.

Andrea, perhaps a little more sensitive to the emotions that Hugo was displaying, set her hand on his shoulder. She seemed to have forgiven him for not telling her about his Russian mother.

'What happened to him?' she asked.

'Murdered by two thieves,' Hugo said. He hated lying, but he could hardly tell the truth about what had happened, so he repeated a line his mother had drilled into him.

'That's horrid,' Andrea said. The sincerity in her eyes made Hugo feel guilty about lying to her. 'Did they ever catch them?' she asked. Hugo shook his head.

'No leads,' he said.

'How did they know it was two thieves?' Andrea asked. Hugo had never had to consider that dynamic before, and he had to think about it for a moment before he answered.

'Two different bullet holes,' he said, 'different guns.'

'That's twisted,' Andrea said disgustedly, 'and in cold blood as well...' she trailed off. Hugo very nearly told her the truth then; he couldn't bear to see her so caught up in a half-fabricated story.

The doors of the director's office burst open and Goebbels came in with Oliver and Lottie.

'I'm still not sure whether you're brave or insane,' Goebbels told him. Oliver shrugged.

'Sometimes there's very little difference between the two,' Oliver said sagely. Goebbels smiled.

'Easy way to find out,' Goebbels said. He walked around the desk and sat behind it, facing Hugo, Lottie, Andrea, Jens and Oliver.

'How?' Oliver asked.

'I exaggerated about what you would be going through,' Goebbels said, 'in fact, if everything goes to plan, you won't meet any Russian soldiers at all.' Oliver breathed a sigh of relief and a smile broke out on his face.

'Oh thank God,' he said, 'I was starting to feel like I was going to die on this mission.'

'What are you talking about?' Jens asked.

'You remember how I didn't think anyone from Fatherland house would want to come?' Jens nodded, 'When I asked, every single one of them put their hand up. It occurred to me they might just be afraid of seeming afraid, so I started to give those details. A quarter of the hands went down when I told them the mission would be in Russia, and after a few more choice details, all but his,' Goebbels pointed at Oliver, 'had gone down.'

'Then he started to say crazy stuff, like we'd have to kill Russian soldiers and we would spend every second being shot at or chased.' Oliver said. Goebbels laughed.

'I did get a little carried away,' he admitted.

'He said all of that and you kept your hand up?' Jens asked incredulously. Oliver nodded.

'Perhaps you are a little crazy,' Goebbels mused to himself.

'You weren't serious though, about the killing Russian soldiers and being shot at, were you?' Jens asked, trying to make it sound like a throwaway question.

'And if I was?' Goebbels asked, suddenly serious. 'No nephew of mine will shy away from a little danger.'

'Just wondering,' Jens said, going a little red. 'What is this mission exactly?' Goebbels made a little bridge with his hands and rested his elbows on the table, suddenly business-like.

'Your mission stems from a simple fact,' Goebbels said, taking a dramatic pause. 'Operation Barbarossa has failed.'

PART TWO:

The Mission

13

Mission briefing

The impact of Goebbels' words was somewhat lost, because only Hugo, Andrea and Jens had any idea what Operation Barbarossa was.

'Operation Barbarossa is the invasion and conquest of the Soviet Union,' Goebbels said when he saw the blank looks on Oliver's and Lottie's faces.

'Oh,' Lottie said. 'I'm sorry, sir. I knew we are invading Russia. I just didn't know it had a name.'

'But Minister,' Andrea said, 'we were told that an advance was made yesterday. How could the operation have failed?'

'Fifty metres,' Goebbels said shortly.

'Pardon?' Andrea asked.

'The advance made was of fifty metres, and it is the only advance that has been made over the last two weeks,' Goebbels said. Andrea was visibly deflated by this news

Goebbels cleared his throat. 'I'm sure you three,' he motioned to Hugo, Andrea and Jens, 'know what Blitzkrieg is.' The three of them nodded, though Hugo did so rather less confidently. 'For your benefit,' Goebbels said, now talking to Oliver and Lottie, 'Blitzkrieg is the way we have fought the war up until now. It relies on quick victories, one after the other. It took us just a month to take Poland; a little over a month to conquer France; and we beat the

Dutch in a week. Do any of you have any idea how long we have been fighting the Russians?'

'Four and a half months,' Andrea said immediately. Goebbels nodded.

'Exactly,' he said.

'But Russia's a far larger country than France or Poland. It should take longer,' Jens said to his uncle, who chuckled.

'That's what our Generals have been telling the Führer for the last three months,' Goebbels said, 'but the fact remains that the distance to Moscow from our stronghold in West Prussia is little more than the distance from the top of France to the bottom.' Oliver opened his mouth, perhaps to suggest something to the contrary, and then thought better of it.

'What are we here for then?' Lottie asked matter-of-factly, 'What on earth can we do to change the course of the war?'

'We feel that the situation could be salvaged if we were to deal the Russians one heavy blow. A flash knockout if you will,' Goebbels said. 'So listen to me very carefully. We want you to kill Joseph Stalin.'

Jens laughed for a very long time after that, and he came close to falling off his chair several times. It was manic laughter; he would stop for a second, catch sight of his uncle, then fall back into tears of mirth.

Once his laugh slowed to a snigger and a cough, Goebbels began to talk.

'I will admit, I had the same reaction when I was told about the scheme,' he said, 'but there is quite a large chance of success if we act quickly.'

'It's absolutely ludicrous!' Jens said, a smile creeping back onto his face, 'his own people barely know where he is, and there are millions of them who'd happily die for him.'

'I agree with Jens,' Andrea said, 'Stalin probably has dozens of doubles as well, to help protect his against assassinations attempts.'

'That's true,' Goebbels conceded, 'but we know pretty much where he will be at any given time.'

'Really?' Jens asked, unconvinced, 'so where is he at the moment then, Uncle?'

Goebbels took a thick wad of papers from underneath the desk and flicked through them. 'Let me see... it's the tenth today... here we are,' Goebbels said, turning the page around so Jens could see. 'He is currently negotiating with British diplomats in St. Petersburg.' Jens took the papers off his uncle and looked over them. Oliver got up off his seat and craned his neck to take a look.

'How do you know it's accurate?' Oliver asked.

'And how did you get it?' Jens asked in disbelief.

'We have spies working all over the world.' Goebbels said, 'And one such spy has spent the last seven years infiltrating the NKVD until, half a year ago, he was made part of Stalin's team of bodyguards.'

'What is the NKVD?' Hugo asked.

'The best way to describe them would be the Russian secret service,' Goebbels explained.

'Why don't you just get that spy to kill Stalin?' Lottie said. 'I'm sure he has a much better chance than we do.'

'Yes, that may previously indeed have been the case,' Goebbels said, 'but unfortunately, at present, the chance of him carrying out the mission are, shall I say, tending towards zero. You see, the Russians tortured him to death at the beginning of the month.'

Goebbels studied them, looking for any signs of worry. 'Besides,' he said, 'Even if he were alive, I think the plan we have for you has a far higher chance of success.'

'What is this plan, sir?' Lottie asked.

'It's quite clever actually,' Goebbels said. 'Look at the appointment listed there.' Jens traced his finger down the page and read:

'Speech at YPOSU camp. Tenth of December.'

'Exactly. That is where you will get him,' Goebbels said. 'It stands for Young Pioneers' Organisation of the Soviet Union. It's very similar to our own Hitler Youth,' Goebbels added.

'So we'll go to this camp thing, Stalin will do his speech, and then... what?' Oliver asked.

'One of you shall shoot him,' Goebbels said, 'from a good distance away though.'

'Who?' Lottie asked, 'I've never handled a gun before.'

'The identity of the assassin will be decided at a later date, but I wouldn't be too worried if I were you, Miss Safin,' Goebbels said. 'This mission has the personal backing of the Führer himself, and he isn't too keen on the idea of a girl assassinating someone as important as Stalin.'

'Why not?' Andrea asked.

'Because,' replied Goebbels, 'the Führer is of course aware that after we win the War, we shall rule over the Russians, and it seems unnecessary for them to hate us even more because of their humiliation that a lovely young German woman killed their beloved Stalin.'

You could easily see the difference between Lottie and Andrea in their reaction to what Goebbels said. Lottie looked relieved, whereas Andrea looked disappointed.

'I'm just as capable of shooting Stalin as anyone!' Andrea fumed. 'More capable even.' Goebbels put his hands up in mock surrender.

'Don't shoot the messenger,' he said. Oliver chuckled.

'Oh ha ha,' Andrea said.

'I'm not joking, Miss Ducasse,' Goebbels said, 'I assure you that if you prove yourself to be the best shot, then I'll have no problem tasking you with the shooting. Despite the Fuhrer's preference, he will not do anything to endanger the mission. The best shot will shoot.' Andrea was visibly appeased, and she relaxed in her chair.

'How are we going to get back afterwards?' Lottie, always the pragmatist, asked.

'Excellent question,' Goebbels said, 'let me see.'

'All right,' Goebbels said, holding a sheet of paper up. 'So listen, a small part of our Third Panzer Army will be passing through a town called Zaraysk two days' after Stalin's visit. It's thirty-five kilometres from the camp and so you'll have to make your own way there.'

'Right,' Lottie said.

'Any more questions?' Goebbels asked.

'They're the only two who can speak Russian,' Oliver said, pointing at Hugo with one hand and Lottie with the other.

'Indeed they are,' Goebbels said. 'Your point?'

'I was wondering how we're going to get around this camp place. People are bound to try and talk to us,' Oliver asked.

'That is probably the most ambitious part of this whole operation,' Goebbels said, 'Hugo and Lottie are going to spend the next three weeks teaching you as much Russian as possible. You'll all be taken out of normal lessons. I have a list of phrases that you will probably need, and let me be absolutely clear,' Goebbels bent down and took five fairly thick wads of yellow paper out from underneath the desk, 'if you are caught speaking German. You will be...'

'Shot,' Jens finished. Goebbels shook his head.

'If only. They will send you to a gulag,' Goebbels said.

'What's a gulag?' Lottie asked.

'Imagine one of our concentration camps,' Goebbels replied, 'only much worse. The average winter temperature at a Soviet gulag is minus forty Celsius. They won't kill you straight away either. They'll torture you into telling them everything you know about Germany and the workings of our great Nazi Party.'

'Jesus,' Jens said, 'those Russians are beyond cruel.' Hugo fought to keep his face still and not let the disbelief show. Goebbels nodded and got to his feet, dusting himself off and looking down at a silver watch on his wrist.

'You have half of today to get started learning,' he said, 'I will be checking up on you in four days' time, and I expect significant progress to have been made. Good luck,' he left the director's office quickly and quietly, leaving Hugo, Lottie, Jens, Andrea and Oliver by themselves.

'I like your uncle,' Andrea said to Jens.

'He's certainly a great man, and a great Nazi,' Jens said.

'So how are we going to sort this teaching thing out?' Hugo asked, careful not to say what he himself thought of Joseph Goebbels. 'Should we teach you together, or split into groups?'

'Oh God, I couldn't teach with you, Hugo,' Lottie said, repulsed by the idea, 'I suggest we split into groups. I'll have Jens if he doesn't mind,' she said casually.

'I don't,' Jens said with a smile.

'That means you only have one person to teach,' Hugo said, choosing to ignore the obvious reason she'd split everyone that way.

'One of us will have to have only one,' Lottie said. 'Oliver, five obviously won't split evenly…'

'Not without a machete, anyway,' Oliver replied. Hugo gave him a withering look.

'Why don't you take two?' Hugo asked.

'Which two should I take?' Lottie asked.

'Since, you want to take Jens so much, have him,' Hugo said. 'And Oliver too.'

'Leaving you alone with Andrea, I see!' Lottie retorted triumphantly. 'See you at dinner!' she added with a smirk, then left with Jens before Hugo could say anything.

Hugo, Andrea and Oliver sat in an awkward silence for a couple of minutes, before Andrea glanced at Hugo.

'Come on then,' she said, getting to her feet. 'Are you going to start teaching us Russian or what?'

14

Sharpshooter

There certainly seemed to be some truth in Oliver's self-professed IQ of a hundred and fifty-seven. He was learning Russian at an incredible pace. Andrea had progressed quickly too, but slower than Oliver, whose green eyes lit up with every new verb and conjugation.

Jens wasn't as good as Andrea was, but he did his best and was making definite progress.

Goebbels had, as promised, come in on Friday to check how they were progressing. Oliver had finished learning the phrases on the yellow sheets half an hour after Goebbels had left on Monday and Andrea had finished a short while after.

A few days after the Russian language teaching had started, Goebbels took Hugo, Lottie, Andrea, Jens and Oliver into the woods and to the Victory house shooting range. Down the range stood about a dozen white cut-outs, each about the height and width of a man, at various distances away from the shooter's position. There was a tall boy waiting for them. The boy's eyes were red and sore – he'd obviously been rubbing them, and had still been yawning when they first saw him. The sight of Goebbels brought him sharply back to focus, and he stood straight as an arrow.

'I have precious little time to decide who is to be our assassin, so I am leaving you in the capable hands of Lutz Roth, a three-bar in Victory house and the best shot at War

School,' it was quite amusing to see such a large boy attempt to supress an embarrassed smile, he looked constipated.

Goebbels nodded twice – once to Hugo, Lottie, Andrea, Jens and Oliver, and once to Lutz, then left.

Lutz signalled them to follow him to their shooting lanes and lie flat on their chests, where a long brown gun was waiting for each of them. Lutz stood behind them, under a small canopy with boxes of bullets stacked behind him.

'These guns are less powerful than the gun the assassin will use,' Lutz said. 'These are all the standard Gewehr 41, but the shooter will use a Karabiner 98k with a telescopic sight.' He seemed to enjoy showing off his knowledge so they hadn't interrupted him.

'So the person that hits the targets most consistently will get the job?' Jens asked innocuously.

'More or less,' Lutz said. 'I'll give you some time to get used to the guns before testing you though. There's plenty of ammunition behind you. You may begin!'

***

'Good shot, Hugo!' Oliver said in slow but accurate Russian. Hugo had just hit the cut-out furthest away from them square in the jaw.

'That was perfect, Hugo,' Lutz said with a hint of approval, 'but perhaps you could work on doing that more than once every twenty minutes.'

Lutz walked down to Jens.

'Jens, can you at least try to hit one of the targets?' Lutz asked, 'your form is almost perfect, just focus and you'll get it eventually.' Jens hadn't hit a cut-out since they'd arrived, almost an hour ago.

'I'm trying to,' Jens said. He squinted through the scope of the rifle and held his breath.

There was a crack and the bullet hit a tree about ten metres away from what he was aiming at. 'See?' he said, 'I'm just a terrible shot.' Lutz seemed to accept this with a sigh.

'Fine,' he said. 'I have a meeting with Mr von Ribbentrop, so I'm leaving the four of you alone for a bit. When I come back, I hope there's an improvement,' Lutz said, making his way from the shooting range and towards the main block.

'What's wrong, Jens?' Oliver asked, 'You haven't got close to anything yet.'

'Seems I'm not too good with guns,' Jens said, sitting on the floor and laying his gun across his lap. Oliver stood and looked at Jens suspiciously.

'No one's that bad,' Oliver said, 'especially not someone with hands as accurate as yours,' he added. Oliver brought the scope of his gun to his eye and fiddled with the adjusting knobs at the top.

'What are you doing?' Jens asked, a flicker of worry in his voice. The other three had stopped shooting to see what Oliver was up to.

'Aha!' he said after a second, taking his eye off the lens and casting an accusing finger at Jens 'you've been missing on purpose.'

'Why on earth would I do that?' Jens asked. Oliver shrugged.

'You tell me,' he said.

'How do you know he's been missing deliberately?' Lottie asked.

'Look at that tree,' Oliver said, pointing down the range. Lottie looked through the scope of her gun in the direction that Oliver was pointing.

'What am I looking for?' she asked. Oliver twisted the adjusters on Lottie's gun for a few seconds.

'Can you see it now?' he asked.

'Oh wow,' she said, answering his question, 'That's quite something.' Andrea and Hugo both got up to take a look.

'Here,' Lottie said, passing her gun to her brother. Hugo pointed it where she had before and looked through the scope at the trees.

On a few of them, there seemed to be a black line that started a foot above the ground and ended a foot before the leaves started.

A closer look told Hugo that the line wasn't a line at all, but a series of holes in the tree. Not one hole was out of line, and the trees themselves were a good twenty metres further away than the target Hugo had hit earlier.

'Did you do that?' he asked. Jens nodded. 'Then you're the best shot here by a mile,' Hugo said.

'Hey!' Andrea said, 'I've hardly missed any,' Hugo handed her Lottie's gun and she looked, 'How on earth...?' she asked.

'I've got very steady hands,' Jens said.

'I suppose congratulations are in order,' Andrea said.

'For what?' Jens asked.

'When we show Lutz that tree, he'll definitely tell your uncle you're the best shot by far. You'll be the one to kill Stalin,' Andrea said.

'You think that deserves congratulations?' Jens asked, 'Being given the honour of killing someone?' He said the word honour with a dark sarcasm that didn't belong in such a nice clearing in such a beautiful wood.

'Don't think about it that way. Think about all the lives you'll save,' Andrea said.

'But I'll still be ending one,' Jens said. 'I don't want to, plain and simple.' Lottie got up and gave him a nudge.

'Remember what your uncle said, about this operation being a failure,' Lottie said. 'If we lose over there, then the Russians will invade Germany.' She looked at Andrea, silently asking if she'd made sense.

'She's right, and the Russians will burn our country to the ground,' Andrea said. Jens looked left and right for a moral ally before Hugo spoke up.

'It's not right,' Hugo said. 'Killing someone shouldn't be the answer to our problems.'

'But it's not just "someone", is it?' Andrea said. 'We're not just ending some random person's life. We're killing Joseph Stalin. That could turn the war back in our favour, and save the lives of so many others.'

'Why do I have to do it?' Jens asked 'Taking that shot won't just be about accuracy, it'll be about nerve. I'll lose focus.'

'I'll do it,' Andrea said immediately. Jens looked disgusted.

'Why are you so eager to end a life?' he asked.

'Because my brother is fighting in Russia at the moment, and anything I can do to make him a little safer I won't hesitate to do,' Andrea said. She hadn't finished, but she was having difficulty with the next bit. 'The thing is, I might miss. You won't if you set your mind to it. It would be better for you to do it.' She looked at him with pleading eyes and Jens looked away, for fear that his resolve would melt.

'I still don't want to,' he said eventually.

Lutz came back to find Hugo, Lottie, Andrea, Jens and Oliver the same way he had left them, shooting down the range at the cut-outs.

Jens was now missing randomly, just in case Lutz noticed what he'd been doing.

'All of you, stop shooting and listen,' Lutz said. They stopped and circled Lutz. 'I've just got off the phone with Dr Goebbels.' He revelled in that for a second. 'He told me to make a decision now, and also how I am to make that decision.' Lutz produced a small box from his pocket, one face of which was adorned with switches, buttons and lights.

'What's that?' Lottie asked.

'It's the controller for the cut-outs. With it, I can make them all go down...' Lutz flicked a switch and the small white shapes in the distance became invisible, 'or make individual ones come up.' He pressed one of the buttons, and the closest cut-out in Oliver's lane came up. 'This is what's going to happen. Each of you will have one shot, and you'll wait for a period of time that will be slightly different for each of you. At some point, I'll make one of the targets in your lane come up and you'll have two seconds to hit it.'

'Two seconds?' Oliver asked, aghast. Lutz nodded.

'We have no idea how difficult the actual shot will be, so Dr Goebbels thought it would be best to make this one as difficult as possible.'

'I have a question,' Lottie asked.

'Go on,' Lutz said.

'Why aren't you coming with us? Surely if you're the best shot at War School, it would make sense to bring you along,' Lottie asked.

'I'm too big,' Lutz said. From the look on his face, Lottie could tell he'd asked Goebbels exactly the same question. 'You have to be taller than a hundred and ninety centimetres to be in Victory house and heavier than ninety kilos. The whole point is that the five of you won't look out of place in this camp, even Jens. I would stick out like a sore thumb.'

'Ah,' Lottie said.

'Any more questions?' Lutz asked. 'No? All right, who wants to go first?'

'I will,' Oliver said immediately. He got into position in his lane and waited.

'Are you ready?' Lutz asked. Oliver nodded.

Oliver grew more and more uncomfortable as time went by, his hands became sweatier and his back tensed up.

When the target eventually came up, it almost made Oliver jump. He pulled the trigger before he had the cut-out in his sights, and the bullet drifted harmlessly away from it.

'Unlucky. Just try to stay calm,' Lutz said. 'Who's next?'

'Me,' Lottie said, lying down in her lane.

'Ready?' Lutz asked.

'Yeah,' she said.

If Oliver's problem was that he was too tense, Lottie's was that she was too relaxed. She trained her gun on the exact place that Oliver's target had popped up and waited; she was extremely surprised then, when the cut-out to its left came up. The two seconds that it stayed up wasn't enough time for her to move her rifle and hit it. Her shot came far too late.

'Bad luck. You shouldn't try to predict where it's going to come up,' Lutz said.

'I'll go now,' Hugo said. He had seen the mistakes that Oliver and Lottie had made and he was sure that he could hit the target.

'Are you ready?' Lutz asked. Hugo nodded.

Hugo waited, holding the gun with firm hands.

The target came up on the left hand side of his lane; he held his breath and fired. It looked like he had missed, but Lutz pressed a button to keep the cut-out up and took out a set of pocket binoculars.

'I thing you might have got it Hugo, well done,' Andrea said warmly.

'She's right, you've clipped its side,' Lutz said, pointing to his own abdomen to indicate the location that Hugo had hit. 'Unfortunately, that isn't a fatal shot. He would be fine with a couple of stitches,' Lutz said matter-of-factly.

Hugo wondered how Lutz could open a sentence about shooting someone and not killing him with 'unfortunately'. He seemed to be completely disengaged from the idea of killing and focused instead on the mechanics of it.

'I'll go next,' Andrea said, getting into position.

There was a cold efficiency in the way she lay down, waited for the cut-out, and then shot it straight through its chest. Hugo didn't like it one bit.

'Fantastic!' Lutz said, clapping. 'You've probably hit the spinal column as well.' Andrea got to her feet and dusted herself off. She looked at Hugo, perhaps expecting him to compliment her shot, and was irritated when he wouldn't meet her gaze. 'Jens, do you want a go?' Lutz asked.

Jens opened his mouth, probably to say no, but the four of them gave him pleading looks. It would be horrible for them to go all that way and for the shot to be missed. If Jens took it, there didn't seem to be any way that could happen.

'Fine,' Jens said. Lutz seemed surprised at how annoyed Jens sounded. Jens got down and he checked the gun, something the other four had neglected to do.

'Are you ready?' Lutz asked.

'Sure,' Jens sighed. The target came up relatively quickly and the second it came up, Jens pulled the trigger. They were all sure he'd hit it, but they only knew where after Lutz looked through his binoculars.

'Straight through the neck,' Lutz said, astonished. 'How...?'

'I was missing on purpose,' Jens said. Lutz nodded slowly, his eyes still on the cut-out.

'I'll need more than one good shot to recommend you,' Lutz said, his astonishment fading away, 'unlikely as it seems, that could have been a fluke.'

'OK,' Jens said.

Lutz made Jens shoot ten more targets, and he hit each of them in exactly the same spot as before. It began to get a little sickening; the target would come up, Jens would hit it in the neck.

His accuracy with the gun was remarkable, but unlike his skill on the piano, this wasn't a thing of beauty. Jens took no pleasure in hitting the targets.

Jens didn't say much after the targets stopped coming up. There was a coldness in his friend that Hugo hadn't seen before, and for the first time he found himself looking up at Jens with fear – he was a machine.

15

Improvising

This was Hugo's first plane flight, and he was loving it. Not because he was moving at five hundred and fifty kilometers per hour, and not because he was six thousand meters above the ground, but because of the noise.

It was loud enough that prolonged conversation between Hugo, Lottie, Andrea, Jens and Oliver wasn't possible, something he was grateful for – Andrea wasn't talking to him because he hadn't congratulated her on her shot, and wouldn't; but it was still quiet enough for Hugo to hear himself think.

The camp they were trying to get to was in a place called Astapova, which was about a hundred and fifty kilometres away from the small runway to which they were currently flying, and about a hundred kilometres behind the Soviet lines. Goebbels had said that Nazi intelligence had found that the small runway was unguarded, but that the runways closer to Astapova were guarded and so totally unsuitable as landing-sites for the plane. Goebbels had only explained how they would be getting from the runway to the camp that morning, and they were all in a pretty bad mood because of it.

'You'll be hiking,' he had said, with the plastic smile of a man attempting a hard sale. Hugo, Lottie, Andrea, Jens and

Oliver made an assortment of groans and moans, and Lottie looked close to tears.

'Couldn't we just fly to the camp?' Oliver had asked.

'No, and I have already explained why not,' Goebbels explained.

Complaints had been thin on the ground after that.

'What was that?' Hugo sat bolt upright. For a moment, the perfect equilibrium of noise had been broken and, for that moment, Hugo was unable to hear himself think.

'Pardon?' Jens saw Hugo's lips move but the words had been lost to the propellers

The noise came again, this time much louder. Hugo jerked his head up to indicate the sound they had just heard as the one he was talking about.

Jens's eyes widened.

'We're being shot at!' he shouted, his voice straining slightly in panic. Hugo hadn't quite heard what Jens said, but his friend's expression told him all he needed to know.

Hugo knew they were in danger, but before he could react, he heard the sound for a third time and a large chunk of the fuselage behind Lottie and Jens tore off, exposing them all to the freezing air outside.

Their screams were swallowed by the gaping hole, falling to the ground along with the woefully thin bit of metal that had once protected them.

Lottie and Jens sprung up immediately, rushing over to the opposite side of the plane and holding on for dear life.

Andrea was a different story. It was as if her wits had been sucked out. She sat staring at the hole; it didn't seem to register.

Reality only really hit her when her seatbelt, a meagre strap around her waist, tore off. Then she screamed.

It was a testament to the scream to say that Hugo could hear it. The air in the cabin was sucked out of the hole away from him, but somehow, her panic and deep, primal fear of death drove the sound of her voice towards him.

To say that Hugo reacted instinctively would be incorrect. His instincts told him to hug the right side of the plane and let Andrea fend for herself, but he found himself doing the exact opposite. He took his belt off and took a nervous step, and another, then another.

Hugo was halfway across the walkway when the laws of physics regained a hold on the world that Andrea's scream had taken away. For a moment, barely a fraction of a second, Hugo wasn't holding onto anything, and he was thrown across the cabin and through the hole.

Almost. He was about as close to falling to his death as he could be, and he was in the ridiculous situation of having attempted to save someone, only to put himself in more danger than the person he was trying to save.

He turned his head around only to get a good look at the sky outside, and he almost vomited. The scariest thing wasn't the height, but the speed. You couldn't see the shapes of the clouds, they all simply blurred together.

There was a bang from the ground, and Hugo had half a second to pray this fourth shot missed before it exploded into the tail wing. The nose of the plane lurched forward, and Hugo, Lottie, Andrea, Jens and Oliver were rewarded with what might have been the dreaded sound of a klaxon, which felt a lot like 'too little too late'.

Hugo was thrown into the relative safety of the seat in front, while Andrea took up the position of near death he'd just vacated.

This time, her scream was deeper. She was completely aware of the danger she was in.

'THIS IS YOUR PILOT SPEAKING. PREPARE FOR A CRASH LANDING, I REPEAT, PREPARE FOR A CRASH LANDING,' the intercom blared the pilot's words around the cabin, and Hugo, who had only just recovered from being hurled into the chair, was ready to ignore his instincts again. He moved with a lot more caution than he had before, and the relief that flooded into him when Andrea's hand was firmly in his made him giddy.

Hugo had hoped that the white plain they were getting closer and closer to was the top of a cloud but, from somewhere deep inside his head, he remembered the season and realised the white was snow. Snow-covered ground.

Andrea could barely walk, and so, what had begun as a noble venture ended with Hugo dragging her across the floor of the cabin to the opposite side, to the chairs away from the hole.

There were only three seats with seatbelts, not enough for them all. Hugo thought quickly. He indicated to Oliver to take one seat, then shouted to Jens to sit in the other. When Jens was about to chivalrously protest, Hugo shouted to Jens, 'Put the belt round you and Lottie!' He sat himself into the third seat, pulling Andrea on top of him, and quickly lengthened their belt to fit round them both. Luckily, it was plenty long enough. 'Hold tight!' he shouted, and they held each other as if one could protect the other from hundreds of tons of wrecked metal. Hugo saw the ground coming towards them, and for a shadow of a shadow of a second, they were close enough to touch it.

The impact catapulted Hugo off his seat, and his seatbelt tore apart in a sorry display of health and safety. The sound of the crash was swept aside by an all-encompassing ringing. It was a piercing, relentless noise that alerted a more focused side of his brain that to come out of the crash unscathed would be a miracle.

The sheer violence of the crash would have overwhelmed Hugo had he not been so numbed by the shock of it all. The fuselage had torn open above his head, opening the inside of the plane up to the heavens. It was as if God himself were inviting them up. A pungent smell snapped him back to the moment. Fuel. The tail of the plane was on fire. They had to get out.

Somehow, his legs unstable and shaky, Hugo fumbled his way to the hole, and climbed out, collapsing on the ground under the weight of his body. Remembering the fire and the smell of fuel, he reached up to help Lottie down. One by one, they all managed to scramble out, helping each other when they needed to. Hugo found himself in charge, shepherding them all far enough away from the plane so that they wouldn't be killed if it exploded. Andrea was so groggy, Hugo had to practically carry her to safety.

The pilot, Hugo thought. The pilot. Hugo knew he would probably be dead, but he wanted to at least check. Alone, Hugo raced back to the burning plane, and saw at once that the cockpit had been crushed to a size too small for the pilot.

Hugo didn't give up when he saw that, though. He rushed to the smashed cockpit and looked through the shattered window. The pilot was there, but his body was crushed and contorted, and the top of his head was missing. Nothing could be done for him. Hugo felt sick, but managed not to be. He had to get away.

But it might be the last chance to get their bags. He grabbed as many as he could from the ground next to the plane and carried them towards the others.

Just as he reached them, there was a dreadful explosion as the plane's fuel tanks ruptured. Hugo felt a rush of hot air from the explosion, and flung himself towards Andrea, who curled herself into the foetal position.

The first thing Hugo saw after lifting his head from where it was buried in the snow was Andrea getting to her feet and looking up at him. He smiled at her, and her eyes lit up when she realised they were all right. They'd made it!

She kissed him, and this time, rather than merely accepting her kiss, Hugo returned it with vigour and confidence.

Oliver allowed them a whole minute before coughing impatiently. When they refused to stop, he walked up to the two of them and tapped Hugo on the shoulder.

'What do you want?' they asked in unison. Hugo's arms were still wrapped around Andrea, and hers were still around him. Oliver pointed to the plane to remind them of what had just happened.

Hugo and Andrea grudgingly released each other.

'The pilot's dead,' Hugo said. 'I saw him.'

They had survived the plane crash. Jens, Oliver and Lottie came and sat next to Hugo and Andrea. Then they just sat looking at each other, enjoying the sensation of being alive. Nearby, partially buried in the snow where they'd been flung, were all the bags with their equipment Hugo had grabbed from the plane.

For the first time in his life, Hugo felt like a hero.

***

'Where are we sleeping tonight?' Oliver asked. It had been too cold and wet to sit in the snow for very long. Jens shifted from foot to foot uncomfortably.

'We were supposed to be camping. Someone at our scheduled landing-place was meant to give us tents and things,' Jens said.

'Why don't we go there then? I'm sure if we just explained...' Oliver said.

'That's not the problem,' Lottie said, getting to her feet now that Hugo had warmed up. 'Both of you, come and look.' She took out the map and they all pored over it.

'The landing-place we were meant to arrive at is here in Chernava,' she said, pointing to a small town on the map, 'but we didn't get that far.'

'How far away do you think we are?' Hugo asked his sister.

'I don't know exactly,' Lottie said. 'After all, I'm not sure where we've come down, but I think we're much too far to walk it today. We need to find somewhere to shelter, or we'll freeze to death.'

'We're going to have to walk through the night,' Andrea said. 'It'll be OK. We have our warm clothes, and the compass.'

'We're in Russia, during the winter. Trust me, it's going to get a hell of a lot colder than it is now,' Oliver said, exasperated.

'We'll be OK if we stick together and keep our spirits up,' Hugo said.

Andrea glanced at him. 'You're right. Let's check our bags and make sure nothing got damaged.'

Fortunately, nothing seemed to have done. Together they had two hundred roubles in notes, a compass (still working), a long-range radiophone (still working), five sleeping bags, three army knives, a YPOSU uniform each and a set of documents they would use when they arrived at the camp. Jens's bag was by far the heaviest, and that was because it housed his dissembled rifle, hidden among various trinkets that a teenage boy would be expected to have.

'The moon's bright tonight.' Oliver said.

'And?' Andrea asked.

'Oliver, that's brilliant!' Lottie interjected, 'We can use the compass, the moon and the stars to work out where we are,' Lottie explained.

Oliver and Lottie got to work. He spent about ten minutes using the map and compass and looking up at the moon and the stars. The occasionally erratic boy was focused and calm, looking at the sky and naming constellations, whilst Lottie relayed map information to Oliver in coordinates, trying to use the sky to find their place.

After a half hour of trial and error, Oliver spoke:

'Good news. There's a town called Krutoye about ten kilometres away from here. We need to walk southwest. Come on, let's go.'

They gathered the things from their bags and put them back in carefully. Hugo did so in slight awe of his sister, who had turned a complete lack of information into a path to follow. Oliver folded the map so the only thing visible was their corner of the world.

'Lead the way,' Jens said to Oliver, and they set off into the night.

16

Krutoye

Oliver held the map and Andrea led them towards the town of Krutoye. Hugo thought she'd recovered well and was behaving as authoritatively as she could to make up for her inaction on the plane. Jens kept falling behind, and so Lottie had taken to walking behind him and encouraging him along. Hugo found himself in the middle of the line, listening to the arguments over directions between Andrea and Oliver in front, and trying to ignore what Jens and Lottie were saying behind him.

Almost two hours of hard walking in the bitter cold brought them to Krutoye, a distinctly quiet town that promised nothing at all in the dark of the Russian winter. They stopped in the deserted centre of the town and wondered what to do. Hugo glanced at his watch; it was almost a quarter past eight in the evening. Not surprisingly, there were no shops open. There was a café nearby but it was shut. Oliver suggested they try to find somewhere to stay. But a moment later Lottie clamped a hand over Oliver's mouth and pointed down the street. A man was approaching them, and he was getting close to being within earshot.

'Don't speak any German from now on,' Lottie said in a loud whisper, 'let Hugo and me do the talking.' Oliver, Andrea and Jens nodded.

The man took about half a minute to reach them.

'What are you doing out here?' he asked.

'We're hiking to Astapova,' Hugo replied warily, 'and we were hoping to buy...' he'd forgotten the Russian word for provisions, but Lottie interjected before his silence went on too long.

'Provisions and a couple of tents,' she said smoothly. 'It's taken us longer to get here than we expected, and everything's shut now.'

The man looked at each of them oddly.

'Yes, well, everything is shut,' the man said. 'You look a little young to be making such a long journey by yourselves. Where are you from?'

Neither Hugo nor Lottie had an answer to that, as after all they'd arrived unexpectedly near Krutoye after the crash. Hugo tried not to show his relief when Oliver spoke.

'We're from Linvy,' Oliver said. Hugo had no idea where that was, but he trusted Oliver to pick somewhere reasonable. Somewhere far enough that the man probably wouldn't know many people from there, but not so far that making the journey to Krutoye in a day was unreasonable.

'Our parents signed us up for a camp in Astapova, and they thought it would be good for us to come together,' Lottie added. Realisation dawned on the man's face.

'Ah. YPSOU?' he asked them. 'I don't look it, but I was a Young Pioneer once. That was ten long years ago though.' Hugo realised the man couldn't be older than thirty, but he looked like he was pushing fifty, with deep lines across his forehead and a hungry look about him. He seemed nice enough though, and they allowed him a moment of reflection before reminding him they were there.

'Um, excuse me,' Lottie said.

'Oh yes. Right, well if you follow me I'll see what I've got,' he said, and they followed him through the streets of Krutoye.

The five friends stood in the man's modest living room, their bags twice as heavy but their hearts twice as light. They had bought enough food from him – brown bread, cheese, some scraggy-looking ham - to last until the end of the week, and a couple of battered tents. It had cost them forty roubles in total, but Goebbels had given them more than two thousand roubles, so they had plenty of money left. Still, Hugo was almost certain they were being ripped off, but he was tired and he wasn't sure his Russian would hold up to a bout of haggling.

The man waved them off with good grace, counting their money as he did so, which seemed to Hugo to make clear the man's priorities.

Which gave him his idea. He drew out another fifty roubles and carefully showed it to the man. 'It's freezing out there,' he said to the man in his best Russian. 'Do you have a shed we could sleep in?'

The man quickly reached out his right hand and grabbed the money. 'I had a shed, yes, but it'll be freezing there. You can all sleep in my basement. And for another fifty roubles, I'll make breakfast for you in the morning: porridge and bread and cheese and hot coffee.'

Hugo glanced at Lottie, who nodded at him quickly. Hugo turned to the man. 'Thanks. OK, it's a deal.'

'How about the fifty roubles?' the man said.

'In the morning, after we've had our breakfast,' Hugo said.

The man looked at them all for a moment, as if he was going to protest, but then he shrugged and said, 'All right,' and led them down to the basement.

It was a manky old place, but reasonably warm and the man brought down lots of old blankets (which smelt of dogs) for them. Hugo slept close by Andrea, Lottie near Jens, and Oliver on the other side of the basement.

'You do understand how much we've just given him for food and a place to sleep, don't you?' Oliver asked. He was still speaking in Russian.

'It doesn't really matter, does it?' Hugo asked.

'Well, we came over here for a field trip back in 1938...' Oliver said.

'You went on a field trip to Russia?' Andrea sounded a little jealous. Hugo noted she'd understood what Oliver had said in Russian, even though she'd swapped back to German. He took a moment to be pleased with her as a student and himself as a teacher

'Yes, we did,' Oliver said, switching back to German when he was sure the man had gone out of earshot. 'You get to do war games. Field trips are one of the only benefits of Fatherland house. We went to Italy in May.'

'What did you do on these field trips?' Lottie's interest had been piqued by the mention of Italy, and she was now paying Oliver full attention.

'When we were over here, we observed how extreme cold affects animals,' Oliver said, 'let me tell you now, it's practically impossible to give horses frostbite.'

'That's disgusting,' Jens said, looking a little ill.

'It wasn't too nice I'll admit...' Oliver started.

'That's bit of an understatement!' Jens said, 'what, did you leave the poor thing outside and wait for it to die?'

'Essentially,' Oliver said bluntly. Jens opened his mouth to express his revulsion, but Oliver continued talking before he could. 'But,' he raised a finger, perhaps to add a little weight to his point, 'the things we found out helped prepare our soldiers for the cold they're fighting in now.'

'Did you have to use animals though?' Jens asked.

'We could hardly use people,' Oliver replied.

'You could have used Jews,' Jens said thoughtfully. Hugo's heart jumped inside his chest, and Lottie's eyes widened, staring at Jens.

'What are you talking about?' she asked, keeping her voice as level as she could.

'Think about it,' Jens mused, 'there are hundreds of thousands, perhaps even millions of Jews in Dachau, Auschwitz and Buchenwald just sitting there, eating food they get for free. Why not put them to use?'

Lottie coughed, loud as a trumpet and sharp as a knife. It was over before the rest of them knew it had started, and in its depths was a sob.

'That's a bit... inhumane, isn't it?' Oliver said.

'Of course it's inhumane,' Jens said sardonically, 'but Jews aren't humans, are they? And even if they are, they barely are. I'll tell my uncle about my suggestion as soon as we get back,' he said.

More coughs. Lottie had turned away from the rest of them, and Hugo could've sworn he saw a tear drop from his sister's eye and into the musty wooden floor. 'Lottie, are you all right?' the genuine concern in Jens's voice only made her cough harder.

'I'm exhausted,' she said, keeping her face hidden and her voice as level as she could. They lay down beside each other, and Jens pulled her in close and she nestled into his arm, warmed by his body and chilled by his ideas. The rest of them, sensing the end of conversation, followed Jens and Lottie's example, lying down in makeshift beds put together from the sheets their host had brought them.

Hugo realised that this was the first time Lottie had shown any awareness of their personal, private situation since they'd left home. The first time, perhaps, she'd realised that she wasn't like the other students. Hugo wanted to comfort her now more than ever.

But he also felt the need to be comforted, and he gave Andrea a soft squeeze, as if he could articulate his struggle by holding her close. She looked into his eyes, sensing that something wasn't quite right. In that moment, if she'd asked what was bothering him, he would have given himself and his sister away and told her the truth. Andrea didn't ask him anything, however, and a mischievous smile crept onto her mouth.

'What is it?' Hugo asked gently. A rogue strand of dark hair had fallen across Andrea's face, and as softly as if he were plaiting grass, he set the strand behind her ear and kissed her on the cheek.

Her smile, even more mischievous, now ran across her face. Hugo, responding to instructions that certainly didn't come from his head, held Andrea closer and kissed her.

This time, rather than her cheek, he was kissing her warm lips; where Hugo had once been soft, he was now strong and passionate. Yet it was Andrea's vigour that always surprised Hugo when they kissed, as if every time might be their last.

When they broke apart, Andrea's hair, which Hugo had made neater with such care, was a mess and her smile no longer promised mischief; instead it betrayed a sheer, unbridled joy.

'I think that answers your question,' Andrea said with a knowing smirk. Hugo still was dazed, and had no recollection of asking anything at all. His glassy eyes and furrowed brow must have made for an entertaining expression, and

Andrea laughed, a sound not unlike wind glancing over chimes, and closed her eyes to sleep.

Before long, the mouth that had produced such excitement in him before, hung slightly ajar, and a quiet snore began to sound out of it. She was beautiful, Hugo thought to himself, and he lay on his back, looking at the ceiling of the basement, wondering how on earth life could get any better.

17

Heading to Astapova

The man gave them great value for breakfast: second helpings of his piping hot, delicious, honey-flavoured porridge and as much bread and cheese and coffee as they wanted. After they'd finished, Hugo and Lottie thanked the man in their best Russian, and Hugo handed over the fifty roubles in banknotes, which the man carefully stowed away in the right-hand pocket of his trousers.

Outside the sun was bright, though Hugo was sure the temperature must have been about ten degrees below zero. Andrea didn't seem to be too focused on the previous night's intimacy, but Hugo could barely think of anything else. They had kissed before, but this time had been different somehow. Perhaps it was because he had initiated it, Hugo mused.

Andrea was very good at keeping herself at the front of his mind; every time she caught his eye, and nobody was looking, she would blow him a kiss that would cause a fresh spark of electricity to surge around his body. She was incredibly addictive.

As they walked away from the man's house, having said goodbye to him, Oliver announced that Astapova was a hundred and eighty-four kilometres away. The other four stared at him incredulously.

'When were you planning to mention this?' Andrea asked, 'there's no way we can walk that far.'

'If we walk at about four kilometres an hour, we should be able to make the journey in just over four days,' Oliver said thoughtfully.

'Are you joking, Oliver?' Jens said. 'There's no way we're going to be able to make that journey in less than a week, assuming we don't freeze to death or run out of food.'

'In Fatherland house we did tests to find out…' Oliver started.

'That was in Germany, Oliver.' Andrea cut across him, 'It's freezing out here and the snow makes walking twice as hard as it would be back home.'

It looked like Oliver would argue about it for a moment before Hugo saw it occur to him that, even if he was right, he could hardly force them to go on a walk they didn't want to.

'At least we've enough to eat,' Jens said. 'The ham he sold us looks very nice.'

'Well, rather you than me,' Hugo said.

'What d'you mean?' Jens said. 'Don't you like ham?'

Hugo shook his head. 'No, I don't.'

'Oh, I see,' said Jens. Hugo wondered if Jens was going to enquire further into why he, Hugo, didn't like ham but he evidently decided not to.

'What do you think we should do then?' Oliver asked, with a glance at Andrea.

'Simple,' Andrea said, 'we need to get a lift.'

'That's a great idea, but where on earth are we going to get one?' Oliver asked her. Andrea thought for a second. Hugo looked at her but tried hard, successfully he thought, not to stare

'Where's the nearest main road?' she asked. Oliver took the map out from his bag and laid it open in the snow.

'That way,' he said.

'How long a walk is it?' Lottie asked.

'Maybe about twelve kilometres,' Oliver replied as he packed the map back up. 'It's a narrow, one-way road but it's the only one that goes from the border to Kazan.'

'Kazan?' Hugo asked.

'A city on the same bearing from here as Astapova, but much further away,' Oliver explained. Hugo, Lottie, Andrea, Jens and Oliver began to walk.

By the time the road came in sight, the sun had already begun its descent towards the horizon, Russian days in December not being very long. A few possibly suitable-looking vehicles went by as they neared the road, but no one had the energy to run and flag one down.

Eventually they found themselves a few feet from the snowy kerb. Oliver, who'd been walking out in front, turned to the rest of the group.

'How do you propose we get someone to stop?' he asked, not directing his question at anyone in particular.

Andrea, seizing the initiative, marched to the side of the road and stuck her arm out.

It wasn't terribly busy, and no one that drove past her slowed at all.

She took each passing car as a personal insult, and by the fourth she was seething.

'I've got an idea,' Lottie said, out of the blue. She walked up to the side of the road, behind Andrea, and pulled her hood down, freeing her brown hair.

Lottie brought her own hood down, revealing her blond locks; she gave Jens a glace as she did, winking at him.

A box-truck had appeared on the horizon, and the effect of Lottie's actions was immediate.

Lottie cringed at the violent screeching of the brakes, but as she relaxed, relief flooded into her body.

'Hugo and I ought to sit in the front,' she said as the truck came to a stop. She turned to the rest of them, 'you all speak Russian with a German accent. It's not too noticeable so long as you keep what you're saying short; anything longer and it becomes really obvious.'

There wasn't time for anyone to argue before the driver's side door opened and a portly, bearded man stepped out onto the snow.

'Hello, we were wondering…' Lottie began, but the man cut her off.

'There is enough space in the back for three of you.' he said, looking Hugo, Lottie, Andrea, Jens and Oliver over like slabs of meat, 'and two seats in front beside me. Where are you headed?'

'Astapova,' Hugo said. The man shook his head and thought for a second.

'I can take you to within thirty kilometres,' he said, 'so long as these two beauties sit in the front.'

He was pointing at Andrea and Lottie, and that made Hugo uneasy for reasons far more disturbing than Andrea's German accent.

'OK,' Lottie said, and the man turned around to get back into his seat, pointing around the side of the truck for the boys' benefit, 'but my friend here is mute. If you try and talk to her she won't be able to reply.' The man looked at Andrea with something resembling pity, and Andrea did her best to maintain a deadpan expression.

Hugo thanked the stars for his sister's quick thinking as he clambered into the back of the truck with Jens and Oliver.

As soon the passenger door closed, the engine spluttered into life and they began to move.

'How long do you reckon we'll be driving, Oliver?' Hugo asked his friend.

'About one and a half hours,' Oliver replied, after a moment's thought.

'I'm going to get some more sleep then,' Jens said in German. Oliver and Hugo shot him daggers and he covered his mouth. They waited silently for a few seconds, praying that the truck's noise had masked the sound of Jens's voice.

When a full minute had passed without the truck slowing, the three boys relaxed.

'Sorry,' Jens said, in Russian.

'Forget about it,' Hugo replied instantly, also in Russian. Oliver took up a position beside a crack in the truck's side and began to watch the featureless scenery go by, and Jens rested his head on his hand and slowly nodded off.

They sat in silence as the truck ate into their journey.

18

Hiking

It was dark by the time the driver had dropped them off, and he didn't wait around to be thanked. He'd beeped the horn once when the truck came to a stop, to tell the boys in the back they'd come as far as he was taking them, and as soon as the back of his truck was empty he'd driven off.

Oliver took the map out to regain their bearings, and Jens rubbed his eyes to wake himself up from what must've been an uncomfortable siesta.

'How was it in the front, Andrea?' Hugo asked.

'It was great,' Andrea replied humourlessly, rubbing her throat. 'God, it feels good to talk.'

'That man was so strange!' Lottie exclaimed, walking over to the two of them. 'He kept saying "You are both very pretty", and he must've been giving us sidelong glances for much of the trip.'

'What a pervert he was,' Jens said before turning to Oliver, who was squinting at the map in the moonlight. Hugo just felt very relieved that the creep in the van was already so far away.

'Oliver,' said Jens, 'which direction do we have to go in now?'

'That way,' he said, pointing at a right angle in the road. 'It's not going to be fun. Thirty kilometres and almost all of them are uphill.'

Hugo groaned inwardly.

'Lead the way then, Oliver,' he said. Oliver got to his feet and began to walk with his friends in tow, the last of whom was Jens, still yawning and rubbing his eyes.

The cold tightened its grip and the wind seemed to bite twice as hard as it had before. But they soldiered on, walking through the night and fighting off the tiredness and the cold, stopping when they were too hungry to go on to eat some of the food they'd bought from the man in Krutoye.

By about five in the freezing morning, Oliver announced that they were now about halfway through the thirty kilometres.

'Thank God for that,' said Jens. 'Half-way, so we only have fifteen kilometres or so to walk?'

'Yes,' said Oliver. 'We're halfway there as the crow flies, but we're going to have to go around a lake at some point. So technically we probably haven't reached exactly...'

'That makes things even tougher,' Lottie said quietly.

'Too tough I think,' Hugo said thoughtfully. He turned to Oliver, who had begun rolling the map back up.

'I think we need to take a break,' Hugo said, 'we need to eat something warm and get ourselves warm.' Oliver's expression gave his opinion away before he could open his mouth.

'Hugo, even with that man's lift, we're behind schedule,' Oliver said pragmatically, 'we need to give a bit of time to integrate into the camp at Astapova or we'll end up getting caught.'

As prudent as Oliver's concerns were, the cold that surrounded them spoke far louder. Hugo, emboldened by the perilousness of their situation, decided to press his case a little further.

'I think we can risk being a little late if it means getting ourselves back up to full strength,' Hugo said. Andrea, unusually quiet considering the magnitude of the discussion, nodded in agreement before wading in.

'If we don't stop we'll be exhausted when we get there,' she began, 'surely that'll make a mistake more likely?'

'Either way, things aren't going to go to plan at the camp. We're going to be tired or late, and I'd rather problem-solve with a full stomach.' Lottie added. Oliver opened his mouth to argue but closed it. He was fighting a losing battle, both against his friends and his own desire to get there on time – he was just as tired and hungry as his friends were.

Oliver reluctantly unrolled the map and lay it out on the snow. The five of them crouched around it, and once Oliver had relocated them, their expressions darkened.

'There's nowhere between here and the camp. It's just open snow,' Jens said, voicing the latest problem to confront them. Jens looked at the map closer, trying to look for a positive, 'it looks like the journey there is slightly downhill though.' Lottie shook his head.

'Uphill Jens, look at the contour lines,' Lottie said bleakly.

'What about there,' Andrea said, pointing to a small village, 'Sugroby I think?'

'Andrea, that's the complete wrong direction,' in saying it, Hugo realised what she already had – it was their best bet.

'If we're going to stop somewhere, that's the only place we really can,' Oliver said, grudgingly echoing Hugo's thoughts. Andrea clapped and got to her feet.

'What on earth are we waiting for then?' she asked, and they followed her example, standing up and brushing snow off their knees with their gloved hands. Oliver lingered on the ground, checking their bearings before packing the map away. He took his position at the front of the group and began to lead his friends towards Sugroby.

'At least it's downhill!' Lottie said.

'Excellent,' Oliver said humourlessly, 'we can go backwards even faster.' Lottie ignored him and instead sidled up to Jens, who, now that their course of action was clear, seemed alone in the company of his thoughts again. Hugo looked back at them, and saw his sister put an arm around Jens. He was worried about his friend, but there was nothing he could do but merely be there for him – and Lottie could do that much better than any of them could.

The walk to Sugroby was a hard, forty-five minute trudge through the snow; but the hope of warmth and food at the end of it made the time fly by.

Hugo was beginning to see the beauty in the Russian landscape, and he imagined that underneath the feet of snow that blanketed the landscape, there were fields of green like those that swaddled his German homeland, frozen forever. It was strangely comforting, and before long, a red-bricked church came into view.

'There it is,' Oliver said, pointing to the church and the collection of small buildings around it.

'This place isn't half as big as Krutoye,' Hugo said. The complaint in his voice was drowned out by the smile on his face – one of the wooden buildings surrounding the church had a rickety stable attached to it and was clearly an inn of some sort.

'Hamlet, town, village, I don't care what we call it!' Lottie said with glee. 'I can't wait to eat something warm.'

Their hunger and tiredness warped their hopes for Sugroby's inn to the point that once they entered the modest, wooden building, they could not help but be slightly put out by the dark and dingy décor. Jens continued to move as if he was freezing cold once inside, long after the inn's fireplace had warmed his friends, and when an old man trudged up to them and spoke, he barely paid the voice any attention.

'Food or board?' he asked monotonously.

'Food,' Oliver said quickly, avoiding the temptation to stay in Sugroby longer than they absolutely had to. The man trudged off, behind the counter of the inn, and the five of them gravitated towards a table opposite the fire.

Jens moved with them, but did not seem to be paying much attention.

'Jens?' Hugo asked, 'Jens you've been silent for ages,'

'You're not still worrying about the mission are you? Jens it's not a big deal,' Oliver said the word mission near silently, and Jens took a second to put his response together.

'Easy for you to say,' he muttered darkly. It occurred to Hugo that over the last few days, Jens's mood had been slowly worsening. He wasn't angry; anger required a fire that he didn't have the energy for: Jens was depressed. The idea of ending another person's life threatened to unhinge him.

Lottie had adopted her now regular position at his side, and though she wrapped an arm around Jens, the tall boy didn't seem to notice her much.

Hugo thought to offer some consolation, but before he could, the old man returned, carrying five stacked plates in one hand, and a bowl of some kind of meaty kebab in the other.

'Shashlik!' Oliver said excitedly, and he took the bowl off the old man and dropped a wad of roubles into his hands. He set the bowl down, and divided the kebabs up evenly onto the plates, 'These are incredible, when we came on our research trip...' but none of them were listening. They had all begun to eat ravenously apart from Jens, who was clearly as hungry as the rest of them, but ate with a methodical neatness absent from his friends.

The sun had begun its descent as they left the inn, but as the ground began to rise in a gentle hill, so did their spirits. They were full, warm and ready for the final leg of their journey. They had thought of using some of their money to stay at the inn, but Andrea had said she was worried about them becoming too well known. She said they should camp instead. They all agreed; knowing that if they were caught by the Soviet police or army and found to be German agents, and not in German uniform, they would all be shot as spies. None of them were at all keen for that to happen. After all, as Oliver pointed out, 'being dead lasts a long time'.

Andrea had decided that, to make finding their bearings easier in the morning, they would make camp by the next road they came across. It wasn't long until the sound of cars reached their ears. They didn't dare to believe that they had reached the road until they saw it, at which point Lottie practically jumped for joy.

The road didn't just represent the end of a long day of walking, it was the first goal that they had completed on the journey, and one should never underestimate the completion of an objective's impact on morale.

The tents were up within the hour, and excluding Jens, who was inside almost as soon as the boy's tent had been erected, the four friends said their goodnights in a sort of reverie. Andrea tried to give Hugo a hug, but she ended up falling into him in the snow. They laughed like idiots for a minute or two before gathering what little composure they had left and retiring to their tents to sleep.

19

In Cold Blood

Dawn swept the night from the sky as the wind sweeps the pavement of leaves. The morning was slightly warmer than the previous one had been. The naked light of the sun was worth an extra few degrees of heat, heat that petered its way down into their legs, and carried them faster than at any other point in their journey.

Hugo, the kissing session with Andrea in the basement still at the front of his mind, was as happy as it was possible to be at minus five degrees. His coat was warm, his shoes were comfortable and he was in good company.

A convoy of black trucks on the horizon threatened to take this happiness away. There was writing on their sides, but they were two far away for Hugo to be able to read it.

Humans are very sensitive beings. We are aware of slight changes in our environment, and we have senses beyond the five that we are taught when we are little. Hugo wasn't sure what it was, but something about the black trucks scared him. He was no longer comfortable in his shoes and his coat felt horribly thin, the sun seemed to dim and the cold was back.

Why, they didn't know, but Hugo, Lottie, Andrea, Jens and Oliver stopped walking as the trucks went by, and Hugo took a sort of comfort in finally seeing the root of his fear.

The trucks had grates on the back, and gaunt, fading eyes looked out at them. Every man, woman and child has a soul, but these poor, poor creatures had been stripped of all humanity until all that remained was their soul; and the soul cannot survive without the body to protect it.

Hugo didn't need to read the writing on the sides of the trucks. These people were the reality of nightmares that had plagued him since his father had died.

'Jews,' the word was printed in Russian on the side of the trucks. Hugo looked at his sister, whose eyes were almost as empty as the prisoners had been.

'Who are they?' Andrea's face was fraught with worry, 'prisoners of war?'

'No they're not,' Hugo said.

'Who are they then?' Jens asked.

'Jews,' Lottie said. The lack of emotion in her voice threatened so much inside her, but she kept her face studiously blank.

'For the Gulags?' Jens asked. Lottie shrugged.

'No idea,' she said. Oliver stopped walking and turned to face them. He wore a knowing smile that unnerved Hugo a little.

'Of course that's where they're going,' Oliver started. 'It's not common knowledge, but the Russians are as ruthless with the Jews as we are.'

'I doubt that,' Jens said. 'I visited Buchenwald with my uncle last year. There are homeless people better off than those Jews were,' Jens looked thoughtful as he spoke, as if remembering a pleasant memory.

'They aren't killing anywhere near as many here as we are at home, but the Soviets treat their Jews worse,' Oliver said, with the air of someone making casual conversation.

'I doubt that as well. The morning of our Buchenwald visit, I had a slice of pie for breakfast,' Jens said.

'Great,' Oliver said.

'I wasn't finished. The paper that it had been wrapped in was still in my pocket when we arrived at the camp. I threw it into one of the bins, and the second it had left my hands this Jewish man fished it out of the bin and licked it clean,' Jens said. Hugo felt like throwing up, Jens was talking about his people as if they were dogs.

'I suppose you're right then,' Oliver said, 'but when we were last over here, the great purge had just ended. There was literally no one left in some of the towns and there wasn't a single synagogue that we saw that hadn't been wrecked.' Jens laughed.

'Say what you want about the Russians,' he started, 'but they know how to treat Jews.'

Lottie began to cry. Her hands covered her face, catching most of her tears before they could fall onto the snow. She tried to stop herself several times, but she no longer had the energy for it, and a facade is very hard to repair once it's broken.

Jens looked more than a little confused. He wanted to console her, but he wasn't sure what to say.

'Lottie, what happened?' he asked softly. She just shook her head and carried on crying.

Hugo felt just as helpless as she did, but he didn't have a breakdown in him. He was more disgusted than upset.

Oliver looked deep in thought, and in a sudden, smooth movement, he picked up Lottie's bag, which had fallen off her back, and opened it.

'Of course,' he said softly.

'What is it?' Jens asked. Oliver looked uncomfortable.

'She hasn't eaten any of the ham,' Oliver said. Jens was now so confused he almost laughed.

'I don't understand. Why is that important?' he asked.

'Can't you see?' Oliver said, 'she's Jewish.'

There was a pause as they all considered the implications of what Oliver had said.

'That's the most stupid thing I've ever heard,' Andrea said. 'They look the most German out of the five of us.'

'True,' Oliver conceded. 'But think about it. Hugo doesn't eat pork, and neither does Lottie; every time Jens starts talking about the way Jews are treated, Lottie has a break-down of some sort. I'm absolutely sure she's a Jew, and if she is, Hugo is.'

'I'm not Jewish,' Hugo said, staring straight into Oliver's eyes. 'Why would a Jew come to War School?'

Oliver walked slowly up to Hugo and spoke in a hushed tone that suggested privacy.

'I'm not going to judge you,' Oliver said. 'Remember the things that we said about the regime back at War School? I don't care if you're Jewish, I'd just like the truth from you.' Hugo's brain was hard wired for denial, but Oliver's appeal was to the heart, not the mind.

'Oh, this is ridiculous!' Andrea said. She turned to face Hugo, who was struck by the intensity of her stare. She was definitely considering it. 'Hugo, tell him how wrong he is.' But Hugo suddenly felt very tired. Tired of lying, tired of having to lie, and tired of keeping up the endless lies that he'd had to tell.

'It's true,' Hugo said.

'Exa...' Andrea had been halfway through turning to look at Oliver when she registered what she'd heard and wheeled back to face Hugo. 'Pardon?'

There was no warmth in her brown eyes now. They were like muddy steel.

'I'm Jewish,' said Hugo, matter-of-factly.

'I don't believe it!' Andrea shouted.

'Well, believe it, because it's true,' replied Hugo in a dull, flat tone. He was relieved not to be lying any more.

'So you're a Jew too?' Jens asked Lottie, and she nodded sadly. Jens seemed to be experiencing some sort of inner conflict, his love for Lottie seemed to be barely keeping his hatred in check. It was a fine balance between the two.

Jens had no such feelings for Hugo.

He strode up to him, and stopped less than a foot away. Only then did Hugo realise how much taller Jens was than him; and a glance into his tempestuous blue eyes reminded him of a day less than two months ago when Klaus had attacked him. It didn't take a very long stretch of the imagination to see this situation following a similar course of events.

'Jens, I...' Hugo started.

'This had better be some kind of joke,' Jens said. His voice sounded mechanical.

'It's not a joke,' Hugo said, looking up into his face. He was relieved to see that there wasn't any anger in his eyes, until he realised there wasn't anything in them anymore. They were emotionless, like those of the assassin had been so reluctant to be.

He punched Hugo in the side of the head. It was a very good punch, and it came far too quickly for Hugo to do anything.

The manner in which he punched him probably said more than the punch itself. It was the same way that someone would stamp on a cockroach, or swat a fly; Jens had no interest in fighting Hugo, he had become something that

155

needed to be eradicated. Anger wasn't driving him. In some recess of his mind, Jens probably felt he was doing the world a favour.

Strong and accurate as the punch was, Hugo stayed on his feet. He was dizzy and could see stars, but he was still on his feet.

Jens grabbed Hugo by the cuff of his shirt and lifted him off the ground. A look at the horizon told Jens a car was approaching. A well-timed throw would have ended Hugo's life immediately.

Then the anger kicked in. It came back into Jens and he realised the car offered a death too quick and too painless for Hugo's crime.

He dropped Hugo onto the snow and collapsed on top of him, before slowly clasping his hands around Hugo's neck.

It was at this point that Andrea realised that Jens was trying to do more than just inflict pain. She put both of her arms around him and attempted to pull him off Hugo.

'JENS! LET GO OF HIM!' she yelled.

Oliver also saw what Jens was doing; he copied Andrea, with more, but still limited, success.

It was clear to both of them that Jens would strangle Hugo to death if he carried on like this.

Lottie seemed to be in a state of shock, partly because her brother was being choked, and partly because Jens had become some kind of callous machine.

She walked over to Jens and put a hand on his shoulder. She had started to cry again, and her warm tears fell onto Jens's back.

His grip loosened and Hugo spluttered. Jens turned up and looked into Lottie's wet eyes.

Then Jens went mad.

He had been about to kill Hugo, because he was a Jew, and Jens had been brought up to think of Jews as the scum of the earth. But here was Lottie, a girl he cared for more than he cared for himself; and she was also a Jew. Hugo's sister, in fact. Did that mean he should want to kill her as well? The thought made him sick.

He released Hugo's neck and his legs pushed him up off the ground. Calling the action standing would paint a false picture. Jens was not in control of himself.

He took one more look at Lottie, and ran off.

There was a long moment in which Lottie decided whether she would stay to check if her brother was OK or follow Jens. They'd stopped Jens killing Hugo, but would Oliver and Andrea help him?

She felt snowflakes fall on her head, and realised that, if the last few days were anything to go by, Jens would be impossible to see from a distance once the weather got going.

Lottie rushed after Jens, who was already becoming an outline in the distance.

20

Moving On

Hugo drifted in and out of consciousness after Jens's hands had left his throat. He could feel the edges of death's embrace, but he stayed out of its grips.

The whole while, Hugo was aware that Andrea was sitting there, next to him. She was crying as if he had died, and he remembered that he was lying on his back, his eyes closed and his body still. He didn't dare move, lest he dipped into reserves of energy he didn't have.

Hugo now had a lot of thinking time, and he tried to decide how he felt about Jens. There was the obvious need for revenge, but he couldn't bring himself to hate him. After all, Jens had been brainwashed by the Nazis.

What Oliver had said at War School made perfect sense; it did all come back to Hitler. There was nothing wrong with Jens; he was a perfectly normal boy except that by malign fate the evil monster Goebbels was his uncle. He was far too caring a person for the things he had just done to be his own doing. It was as if someone had written a code into his subconscious that turned him into a monster when it was triggered. Calling it brainwashing took away from the subtlety of it, and Hugo was in a sort of sick awe at the skill with which it had been done not just to Jens, but to most of the people in Germany.

Hugo's body had recovered a little more in the thinking time, and he was able to sit up in the snow.

Almost as soon as he had moved, he felt a rush and there were two arms around him. The part of his brain that was still waking up thought that Jens had come back to finish him off, but a saner part, and her voice, told him it was Andrea.

'Jesus Christ, Hugo,' she said, half-angry half relieved, 'I thought he'd killed you.'

'He almost did,' Hugo said. Andrea released him slowly, as if she were worried he would fall back onto the ground.

There was a myriad of emotions in her eyes. She was happy he was alive, but angry he was a Jew; she was worried about his well-being, but she also felt like he had deserved a little of what he'd got.

'Are you all right?' she asked carefully.

'Better,' Hugo said, 'still a bit dizzy.' Andrea sat and waited for a few more seconds.

'How about now?' she asked.

'It's fading,' Hugo said.

'Good,' Andrea said. She looked down into the base of her palm for a moment, and then slapped him.

It left Hugo's ears ringing, and he glared at her. She glared straight back at him.

'How could you?' she asked.

'If you want me to apologise for being a Jew, you're going to be disappointed,' Hugo said stubbornly. Andrea sighed in a very irritated way.

'I don't care about that,' she said. Oliver sniggered. 'Shut up,' she spat. Oliver put his hands up.

'Just ignore me,' he said, fighting to keep his smile under wraps. Andrea turned back to Hugo.

'I don't care so much about you being Jewish,' she said, 'but you should have told me before.'

'Told you I was a Jew?' Hugo asked sarcastically. 'Surely you're not serious? Don't you understand that the only reason Lottie and I are alive is that we haven't told anyone. You have no idea at all. My dad died to keep our secret safe, and you...'

'You told me he was killed by thieves,' Andrea said quietly. Hugo stopped talking immediately.

'Telling the truth about that would've meant telling you the truth about everything,' Hugo said.

'Oh what a terrible thing!' Andrea exclaimed, 'telling the truth!'

Hugo hadn't noticed a change, but she was now standing up, and the snow swirling around her made her look even more impressive and beautiful.

'You don't know what you're talking about,' he tried to sound cold, but it came across as pleading.

'You're right. I don't know what I'm talking about because everything you've told me about yourself is a lie!' Andrea yelled.

'That's not true,' Hugo said.

'Really? What little shred of truth did you forget to rip out of the crap you were telling me?' she asked.

'That I love you,' Hugo said. He'd read that line in a million books, and there was always a grin on his face as he did. It never failed to sound stupid, but at this moment in time, it was the only true thing he could bring himself to say.

He saw her cheeks go red, and he saw her brow furrow as she decided whether he meant it or whether he was lying to defuse the situation.

'You've never said that before,' was what she decided on.

'And I'm sorry I haven't, but I swear it's the truth,' Hugo said. Andrea sighed and sat down in the snow.

They were quiet for a long while. Andrea couldn't think what to say and Hugo didn't want to risk saying anything else.

'So let me get this straight,' Andrea said, 'You're a half-Russian Jew?'

'Yes,' Hugo said.

'But if you and Lottie are Jewish, why didn't the authorities arrest you and deport you to a concentration camp?' Andrea asked.

'Because of my dad,' Hugo said. 'The information about who was Jewish and who wasn't was stored on punched-cards in machines called tabulators. They were invented in America, before the War. My father knew all about those machines and, a few years ago, when he knew what was going to happen to us once the Nazi government began persecuting the Jews; he went one night to break in to the tabulator office in Hamburg. He'd planned to find the punched cards relating to our family, and make changes to the cards so they no longer recorded our religion.'

Hugo drew a quick breath. 'Dad never came home. He was shot dead by a guard at the tabulator office. We never knew for certain if he'd succeeded in his mission. We never knew that. But... the Gestapo never came for us... and so I suppose he must have been.'

Hugo was almost in tears.

'Oh, God,' Andrea murmured, 'your dad was so brave, Hugo. So brave.'

'Yes,' said Hugo.

The two of them just looked at each other.

'So are we good now?' Hugo asked warily. He half expected her to start yelling at him again, but she looked thoughtful.

'Yes,' she said with a wry smile that became stern before it could stretch into a grin, 'Hugo, you'd better not lie to me again.'

'I won't,' Hugo said. Andrea came and sat next to him on his left, and Hugo put a wary arm around her shoulders.

'I hope your sister's all right,' she said.

'Jens as well,' Hugo said.

Andrea turned to look at Hugo. 'She gave him a quick, but wet, kiss on his left cheek. 'You're... you're as brave as your dad was,' she said.

They sat contentedly for what felt like hours, keeping each other warm.

'I'm glad you've made up, but we've got a bit of an issue,' they turned instantly at the sound of Oliver's voice behind them. It was difficult for them to admit, but in the midst of their drama, neither Hugo nor Andrea had noticed their friend's absence.

'What's the issue?' Andrea asked.

'I was searching for an hour, and I've still got no idea where Jens and Lottie went,' Oliver said.

Lottie was a shivering pool of regret. She'd left her brother to pursue the very person who'd attempted to kill him – he might have even succeeded, she had no idea – and not to seek revenge.

She'd just stood and watched as Jens had strangled him, and all she could bring herself to do was touch his shoulder. She remembered a time in the past, before they'd come to the school, When Klaus had attacked her brother. She could've stopped it that time too...

Andrea and Oliver had tried to get him off, but Lottie hadn't. Her own brother.

She didn't think it was possible for her to feel any worse than she did. She followed the tracks Jens had left in the snow for what felt like hours, and it got harder and harder as the snow fell heavier.

She stopped. Where were the footprints? For the first time in a while, she scoured the ground for a trace of them. She spotted something else and gasped.

There was blood on the snow.

She stared at the red drops for several minutes as if, somehow, not believing in their existence would make them disappear. But they stayed there.

Lottie couldn't see how it could be anyone but Jens's blood'.

He must've done something to himself; he hadn't been bleeding. Lottie couldn't see any object that could've done it. Then she found it, the thing that had caused his injury.

She was glad, in a sick way, to find a bloody bayonet sticking out of the ground.

At least she didn't have to look for footsteps anymore. She could just follow the trail of blood Jens had left.

Each splatter of it was larger than the last, and there were bigger bits of it where Lottie guessed he had stopped walking now and then.

A while later, Lottie saw something resembling a barn in the distance. It looked about as welcoming as a cemetery, but Lottie guessed that was where he had gone.

The trail of blood agreed with her, and it led straight up to the barn's door, which was ajar.

She stepped inside.

'JENS!' she shouted, 'ARE YOU IN HERE?'

Lottie heard the faintest whisper of a moan, and she rushed towards it.

Jens was lying in something that might have resembled a haystack a while ago, and Lottie could see where the bayonet had gone through his foot.

She kneeled at his side and caught his gaze. Jens's face was pallid and weak, and the blood that had seeped from his foot had left him on the very edge of consciousness.

'Jens...' Lottie said.

'Lottie, I'm so sorry,' Jens said. She had to think for a while before she understood what he was talking about. It sounded as bad as Lottie felt, but she had almost forgotten Jens might've killed her brother, the brother who'd always protected her growing up. The sight of his blood shocked her, and her mind was fraught with that rather than the sequence of events that had sent her on this journey.

'You can't change it,' she said. Lottie surprised herself; she wasn't usually this quick to forgive.

The little colour that was in Jens's face faded.

'So is he...' he looked around helplessly, 'did I...'

'I don't know,' she said.

'I think I did,' Jens said. A tear fell from his cheek, and as he moved, she saw for the first time his face was shiny and wet. 'I would have sat there and finished it completely if you hadn't stopped me.'

'I didn't do anything but touch your shoulder,' Lottie said. Jens shook his head.

'You reminded me you were a Jew as well,' Jens said. 'It's hard to explain what that did, but I couldn't keep strangling him.'

'Why did you run off?' Lottie asked.

'I was confused. I could hardly believe what I'd done and I couldn't stand that you would hate me for it,' Jens said.

'Where were you going to go?' Lottie asked him. Jens shrugged.

'I was just going to keep walking until I couldn't anymore, and then... I don't know. I was so messed up in the head, I wasn't really planning anything,' Jens said.

'Right,' Lottie said.

'Can I ask a few questions now?' Jens asked, lifting his head so he could look in her eyes.

'Go on then,' Lottie said.

'Why on earth did you follow me? Are you insane?' Jens asked. His face had gained a little colour, and Lottie was inclined to keep making him angry so more would come back.

'You would have followed me,' Lottie said curtly.

'That doesn't matter! It's bloody freezing out there, and what if you'd gotten yourself lost?' Jens asked.

'So I'm not supposed to do for you what you would do for me?' Lottie asked.

'No,' Jens said.

'Why?' Lottie asked. Jens could hear the challenge in her voice, and he was very careful about what he said next

'Because I'm...' Jens started

'You're what?' Lottie snapped. She'd been full of care a few seconds ago, but now she was livid.

'Well, I'm stronger than you,' Jens said. Lottie laughed

'Your arms might be, but you were just telling me how you were messed up in the head,' Lottie said, 'and you almost killed someone in cold blood.'

'What do you mean almost?' Jens said.

'I like to think positively,' Lottie said. 'He coughed when you let go. That has to be a good sign, doesn't it?' Jens gave her a weary look and spread his arms wide.

'What about this situation is positive in the slightest?' Jens asked.

'I think you should think positively,' Lottie said.

'Why?' Jens asked.

'Because if you've killed my brother, I'm never talking to you again, ever, no matter what you say,' she paused to think, 'and I'll very likely do my best to kill you too,' she added flatly. Jens was shocked, but he knew that he really had no right to be, and that she meant what she said.

Jens was silent.

Lottie clapped her hands together.

'Let's take a look at this foot shall we?' she said.

Jens complained endlessly as Lottie took off his shoes, which smelled horrible, and his socks, which were worse.

She looked through his bag for something she could use to clean the wound. After so long dreading the sight of it, it didn't look too bad. The wound hadn't gone all the way through his foot, but Lottie knew it would get infected if she left it how it was.

'Wiggle your toes,' Lottie said to Jens.

'What?' he asked, confusion strengthening his voice.

'I want to see how bad it is.' She replied. Jens didn't press the point and his face strained as his toes clenched and unclenched.

That was a relief. Lottie suspected that had he not lost as much blood as he had, he would have been able to walk.

Lottie stepped over to Jens's bag to look for something that would help her clean his foot. Inside, underneath the concealed gun and the YPOSU uniform she found a small bottle of vodka. Lottie didn't know if they had all had one, or if it was just Jens that had, but she assumed it had come from the man in Krutoye.

It was a little strange actually, why would they have been given vodka?

The bottle's presence puzzled Lottie until she found a green first aid bag. It was open, and further digging rewarded her with a large roll of bandage.

She was a little cruel with the vodka, putting a fair amount more on the wound than she needed to. Jens yelped like a kicked dog, and if he'd had the energy to shuffle away from Lottie, he would have.

'What's that?' Jens asked through clenched teeth. His voice sounded a little stronger.

'Vodka,' Lottie said. 'The alcohol in it will clean the wound.'

'Right,' Jens said, wincing. 'You couldn't use a bit less of it could you?'

'I think I've used enough,' Lottie said, before pouring a tiny bit more into the gash.

'Hey!' Jens yelled.

'Stop being such a cry-baby,' Lottie said, 'and I'd rather your foot stung now than you had to get it cut off later.'

'I suppose so,' Jens said, realising how weak a position he was to argue from.

'I'll try and wrap it in the bandage or something,' Lottie said. Jens nodded.

She had no idea how to bandage a wound, so she wrapped the bandage around Jens's foot until she couldn't see any blood seeping through. She wasn't sure how to fasten it, but she remembered being in hospital a long time ago, and seeing a nurse rip the end of the bandage before tying it around a wound. She couldn't rip it, but found a small pair of scissors in his bag and cut it. Soon she pulled the ends tight.

'Is it done?' Jens asked. His voice was a little hoarse after the surprise of the vodka.

'As well as I could do it,' Lottie said, putting away the excess bandage, 'which means badly.'

'What now?' Jens asked, sitting up.

'I think we should aim to get back to the road as soon as possible,' Lottie said, getting to her feet.

'I don't know if I'll be able to walk on this foot,' Jens said. Lottie's eyes narrowed.

'One moment,' she took the knife from Jens's bag and walked around the inside of the barn. She found a suitable beam and sawed it off.

'What are you doing?' Jens asked. Lottie handed him the beam.

'Merry Christmas,' she said humourlessly. Jens used it to push himself off the ground, and he took a few careful steps with it.

'You know, some people would offer me their shoulder to lean on,' Jens said as they walked out of the barn.

'Some people would have left you to die,' Lottie said.

Jens didn't say anything for a while after that.

The snow had stopped falling, but that only served as a reminder of how lost they were. The two of them followed Jens's trail of blood until it stopped, and they made a wordless decision to keep walking in the blood's direction.

A few minutes after that, Lottie heard a voice

'Did you hear that?' Lottie asked.

'Are you talking to me?' Jens asked.

'Don't be a brat,' Lottie said. 'Let's wait and see if we hear it again.'

The two of them were very close to giving up waiting, and continuing to walk, when they heard it again.

They eagerly followed the sound, and Lottie cupped her hands to her mouth

'Who's that?' Lottie shouted.

'Shouldn't you have asked that before we started going towards whoever it is?' Jens said. Lottie swatted at him.

'Who else is it going to be?' Lottie asked.

'That barn has to belong to someone,' Jens said, 'and that sound might have been a Russian calling for his husky,' Lottie didn't say anything, because she was still angry with him, but Jens was right.

'Who's that?' she shouted in Russian this time, and she heard a response immediately.

'It's Oliver! Where are you, Lottie?' the voice yelled back. The two of them followed the sound of Oliver's voice as quickly as Jens's foot allowed.

'Is Hugo all right?' Lottie shouted. There was no reply.

A couple of hundred metres later, two figures started to come into sight.

One of them was sitting down and the other was standing. The standing figure caught sight of them and waved them over.

'Lottie!' it was Oliver, 'and you found Jens,' Oliver's scowl was a work of art. It suggested utter and complete contempt without being an eyesore; it was as if he'd practised it.

'Where's my brother?' Lottie asked.

'He's...' Oliver stopped scowling and looked down at his shoes, 'do you want to see him or should I just tell you?'

'Oh God,' Lottie said, she pushed past Oliver and stopped dead in her tracks.

Andrea was kneeling next to Hugo's body, her face in her hands.

There was something unnatural about the way Hugo was spread on the snow.

'He almost survived it,' Oliver said.

'What do you mean "almost"?' Lottie didn't turn around. She just stood, transfixed by the sight of what she had supposed to be her brother's corpse. But, she couldn't take it in. Not at all. She'd been so sure he'd survived.

'He was awake for about five minutes after you ran off after him,' Oliver said him as if it were the worst insult in the world, as he gestured at Jens, 'but then the snow got a whole lot worse.'

'What happened then?' Lottie said dully. It was slowly sinking in that she was now an only child.

'He was really weak,' Andrea was talking now; every word was punctuated by a choke or a sob. 'We couldn't get him warm quickly enough.'

'He passed out again a few seconds after the snow receded,' Oliver, who walked around to face Lottie, continued, but she didn't look away from Hugo.

'The last thing he said to us was that we should finish this mission,' Oliver said. 'He also told us to forgive him,' he gave a sharp nod towards Jens, 'and we should say he died in the plane crash so Jens wouldn't be convicted.'

Lottie couldn't help thinking something was not quite right. She'd been staring at Hugo's face the whole time, and it looked to her like the corners of his mouth were coming up.

'He's smiling,' Lottie said softly. Oliver shook his head sadly.

'It's called risu mortui. It means smile of the dead in Latin,' Oliver said sagely. Lottie looked up at him, confused.

'How does that work?' she asked.

'The muscles in your face that make you smile are extremely quick to expand and contract,' Oliver said. 'If someone dies in a cold place, the muscles in their face contract from the cold faster than the rest of the body, and it makes them look like they're smiling.'

Lottie looked back at Hugo.

It seemed to her he looked as if he was trying to hold back a smile rather than his facial muscles unnaturally contracting.

'It looks a lot like a smile to me,' Lottie said. Oliver shrugged.

'Perhaps it's a sign,' Oliver said, a touch rushed. 'Maybe he's smiling on us from above.'

Realisation hit Lottie like a train. She gave Oliver her saddest look before stamping on his foot as hard as she could.

Oliver howled in pain and grabbed his foot.

Lottie marched up to her brother and kicked him in the ribs.

Hugo made a similar howl and sat up, rubbing his side.

'How could you?' she yelled.

'It took a lot of planning actually,' Oliver said. 'You took ages to come back, so we thought we'd have a little fun.'

'A little fun?' Lottie said hoarsely. 'A little fun?' Jens saw the funny side a lot faster than Lottie did, probably because he was no longer a murderer.

'That thing you said, what does it actually mean?' he asked Oliver

'What, risu mortui?' Oliver said, 'it means smile of the dead. I think. It was a hasty translation.'

Lottie still looked aghast.

'I probably should've seen this coming from you,' Lottie said, pointing at Oliver, 'and my brother's an idiot; but Andrea?'

Andrea put her hands up.

'They practically forced me to do it,' she said. Hugo cast an accusing finger at her.

'It was basically your idea!' Hugo said. 'You kept pointing out problems during the practice.'

'You had a practice?' Lottie asked.

'Three of them,' Hugo complained, putting up three fingers to emphasise the largeness of the number. 'She said I was the worst corpse she'd ever seen.'

'Well it was your smiling that gave it away in the end,' Andrea pointed out.

'That's not true, it was Oliver's smiling from above line,' Hugo said.

'I wouldn't have had to say it if you could keep a straight face,' Oliver retorted. 'And you wouldn't have had to keep a straight face if we'd just followed my plan.'

'Which was?' Lottie asked, curiosity finally getting the better of her outrage.

'I wanted to bury him,' Oliver said, a little too wistfully for Hugo's liking. 'I'd have done a little funeral eulogy in the snow as well.'

Lottie thought for a second.

'You could've just sent him off a couple minutes that way,' Lottie said, pointing into the distance. 'He'd have been invisible that way.' Oliver slapped his forehead.

'That's brilliant,' Oliver said. 'That would've worked so well.'

'And I could have approached out of the dark, like a ghost or something,' Hugo said. Oliver nodded.

'If only we'd had you in the planning stage,' he said.

'I think we ought to start walking now, don't you?' Lottie asked. There was a mumble of vaguely positive noises, and they picked their bags up and prepared to walk.

'Which way, Oliver?' Jens asked.

Oliver looked down at his compass, and he pointed down the road.

'That way,' he said.

Lottie slowed her walk until she and Hugo were walking next to each other.

'I suppose I ought to say thanks,' Lottie said reluctantly. Her voice was just loud enough for Hugo to hear.

'Why?' Hugo asked.

'I don't think I had an emotional reunion in me,' Lottie said, 'that whole thing took the edge off.'

'You're welcome I suppose,' Hugo said, 'and I owe you a thanks for getting Jens off me.'

'I didn't really do anything,' Lottie said meekly. Hugo shrugged.

'All I know is that he stopped when you asked him to. It doesn't really matter what you did, it worked better than anything else,' he said.

'Andrea and Oliver were actually doing something though,' Lottie said, wallowing a little, 'I couldn't bring myself to do anything to him.'

'Oh,' Hugo said. That seemed to shock him a little bit, 'even though he nearly killed me?' Lottie shook her head.

'I'm not having this argument with you now,' she said.

'Why not? Scared you'll hurt Jens?' Hugo said, his voice raised.

'That was low,' Lottie said.

'No it wasn't. Low is being torn between your brother and a boy you've only known for a couple of months,' Hugo said. He hadn't realised he was this upset with her, and he wasn't in any mood to hold back.

'You said it didn't matter what I did,' Lottie said

'I didn't know you'd stood there thinking about it!' Hugo shouted. Lottie was of half a mind to concede and apologise. She could count on one hand the number of times he'd been this angry with her.

But it struck her that he might not forgive her if she said sorry, it wasn't as if it was a small thing she'd done.

'You're being completely unreasonable,' Lottie said.

'Is it unreasonable for me to want my sister to make a decent attempt at saving my life?' Hugo said. 'And it's not as if you stayed behind to see if I was alive or not. The second he let go and ran off you chased after him!'

'What if the situation was switched around?' Lottie asked.

'What are you talking about?' Hugo asked.

'If Andrea was strangling me, what would you do?' Lottie asked. Hugo was about to say something, then caught himself. He paused and thought for a second before he spoke.

'That's not the same,' Hugo said. Lottie folded her arms and smiled gleefully at him.

'Oh really? How?' she asked.

'That wouldn't happen because Andrea's not crazy like Jens is,' Hugo said flatly.

'Pardon?' Jens said. Hugo turned to face him.

Hugo, Lottie, Andrea, Jens and Oliver had stopped walking. Oliver, Jens and Andrea had been listening to the situation escalate.

'I think you'd find it pretty hard to make an argument for your sanity,' Hugo said curtly, 'seeing as you can't bring yourself to kill a mass murderer but you'll happily strangle me, apparently a friend, to death.'

Jens stared straight at Hugo, as if he could beam what he was thinking through the air and into Hugo's head. His fists were balled inside his pockets, and Hugo assured himself that he would make a fight of it if the situation escalated.

'Wait,' Oliver said. They all turned to face him. He strode up to Hugo and looked straight into his eyes.

'What are you doing?' Hugo asked. Oliver didn't reply, his green eyes looked over Hugo's several times before he said anything.

'As I thought,' he said, 'you haven't completely recovered.'

'How?' Hugo asked. Oliver scratched his chin.

'I don't know, do I look like a doctor?' he asked. 'Your eyes are a bit wobbly and you're blinking a lot.'

'Well what does that mean?' Hugo asked.

'It means you're not really thinking things through,' Oliver said. 'You wouldn't have said that stuff to your sister otherwise.'

'But I feel fine,' Hugo said. Oliver thought for a second.

'You know Jens?' Oliver asked.

'I haven't lost my memory,' Hugo said.

'That's not what I was going for,' Oliver said. 'What would happen if you were to fight him?' Hugo looked Jens up and down carefully.

'I think I...' Hugo began.

'Wrong. He would beat you to a pulp. The fact that you don't remember how he picked you up with an arm a few hours ago proves I'm right,' Oliver said.

'What do you recommend?' Hugo asked.

'I think you should walk ahead of us for a while, so you don't run your mouth anymore,' Oliver said. Hugo nodded, suddenly docile, and strode to the front of the group and down the road. Oliver smiled to himself.

21

Young Pioneers

'There it is,' Oliver said.

He pointed to a large building that resembled a fort. It looked old but had evidently been maintained well, and it was magnificent in comparison to the dull landscape surrounding it.

The only thing remotely interesting in the surrounding area was a sparse spinney, a couple of hundred metres to the right of the main building. The spinney was mostly full of leafless trees, but there were a few tall dark green pines too.

'Should we get changed into uniform then?' Andrea asked. Hugo took his hand out of its glove and his fingertips went pink from the cold in seconds.

'I think we should wait till we get there,' Hugo said, replacing the glove. They continued to walk, and before long, they were standing in front of the camp.

The building was far larger than it had looked, and a metal gate took up a good quarter of the front face.

Beyond the gate, Hugo, Lottie, Andrea, Jens and Oliver could see children of different ages walking around. Some of them held ice skates and the smaller ones were chasing each other around. All of them wore the YPOSU uniform, a white shirt with a red neckerchief. It reminded Hugo of War School a little.

'Oi!' shouted a voice from their left in Russian, 'what are you lot staring at?'

They turned around to see a man glaring at them so intently that his scowl was visible despite him being a hundred or so metres away. He was stood outside an extraneous little hut that sat at the bottom of the fort's walls and made it look uneven.

'We're part of the Young Pioneers,' Hugo said. The man folded his arms over his considerable gut.

'Really?' he said. Andrea took a mental note of the man's tone, sarcasm is slightly different in every language and she didn't want to sound like an idiot if she ever attempted it, 'Well I don't believe you, how about that?'

'We've got documents that prove it,' Oliver said. He reached a gloved hand over to Jens's bag and relieved him of it. His hand went around the dissembled gun and the medical kit and eventually found a brown envelope.

The man looked disappointed, he obviously had a few quips left in him and the envelope had taken the wind out of his sails.

'Come on and let me mark you off then,' he turned and went back into his hut.

It was as homely as you could expect it to be, which is to say it wasn't homely at all. The only thing moderately pleasant about the hut was that it was warm.

'Here you are,' Oliver said, handing the man the envelope. He looked around the room as he opened it and thumbed through. One of the walls had a portrait of Stalin mounted on it. The similarity between it and the image of Hitler in Hugo's room was uncanny.

'All of this seems in order,' the man said, getting to his feet.

The rooms at the camp seemed to Hugo to have been designed with them in mind. There was enough space for Hugo, Lottie, Andrea, Jens and Oliver to relax in comfort, even though the room was for the three boys, and the door could only be locked from the inside. The girls hadn't yet gone to their room, and their bags were still piled up in a corner.

Once they were sat and comfortable, Jens, who'd been lagging while walking lately, commented how cold the room was. The culprit was a large window opposite the door, which had been left slightly open. Andrea strode over to it and banged it shut. They were on the second floor of the building, though the snow made it difficult to tell exactly how high it was.

'Hello?' there was a knock at the door.

'Yes?' Lottie said.

'You have a meeting with the camp's supervisor,' the voice said.

'One second,' Lottie said. They all got up and straightened the uniforms they'd donned, before Lottie strode to the door and unlocked it.

'Good, you're ready. Let's go,' the person had sounded female but they hadn't expected a little girl of barely twelve. Jens was at least half a metre taller than she was and it was humbling for them to have to follow her around.

The supervisor's office was on the other side of the camp to their rooms, and so the walk took them around the camp. The building did seem to be an old fort, what with the large courtyard in its middle and the portcullis-like gate on one of its façades.

'Here we are,' she said. They stopped walking outside a door that was bland compared to the others. The little girl

178

rapped the door three times with her knuckles, before giving them the vaguest of nods and skipping away.

'Come in,' said yet another new voice. They opened the door and took in the supervisor's office. The most colourful thing inside it was the red soviet flag in one corner. It had a brass stand and looked to be made from velvet.

There were five chairs in front of the supervisor's desk, and it probably said a lot for the size of the desk that even with spaces between each of the chairs the desk still outflanked them.

'Good afternoon,' Hugo said. The man barely looked up from his desk.

'Afternoon,' he said, 'sit down then,' he put a hand out to indicate the five chairs in front of his desk. They sat down.

'It's really good to finally be here,' Lottie said.

'I hope you'll enjoy your time here, and I also hope you'll be helping set up the camp for our special guest,' the supervisor said.

'Oh yes, we heard about...' Hugo started. Lottie and Oliver gave him a death stare and he stopped talking immediately. The supervisor looked up, now paying them the closest attention.

'You heard about what?' he asked sharply.

'We heard some of the other pioneers talking about setting up for something,' Hugo said, measuring his voice so he didn't sound rushed. The supervisor relaxed his shoulders, but his eyes were still narrowed in suspicion.

'This was after you had arrived here, correct?' he asked. Hugo nodded.

'Fine,' the supervisor said. He went back to sorting through the papers on his desk. 'I am extremely busy, so if that is all...'

'Can I ask who this special guest is?' Lottie asked. The last traces of suspicion faded from the supervisor's eyes as he looked up at Lottie.

'Joseph Stalin,' he said. They all did their best stage gasps and the supervisor looked a little mollified. 'All right, off with you.'

They got up and left the office, leaving the supervisor alone to finish his paperwork, which seemed to grow as he progressed with it.

22

Joseph and Dmitri

Dmitri Markov was one of the most powerful men in Russia.

Right now, he was on his way to meet one of the very few men in Russia with more influence than he had.

Dmitri passed countless checkpoints as he walked towards the Kremlin Senate, a deceptively plain building on the edge of the Kremlin, the fortified complex in the heart of Moscow. Not one of the men at the checkpoints asked Dmitri who he was or what he was doing. The checkpoints were ineffectual for the most part. Anyone who got into the Kremlin had a reason to be there.

The Kremlin Senate had three doors, and it was a tradition of Dmitri's to walk through the right one every fifth visit. He pushed it open and strode inside.

There was a staircase straight in front of him, flanked by two soldiers. Dmitri did not climb it. This staircase was the last line of defence against a possible intruder. The soldiers had explicit orders to shoot anyone that took more than two steps up it.

Instead, Dmitri turned right, following a near invisible hallway and going up a narrower set of stairs. At the top of the stairs was a door with a red star on it. He did not knock. It had been decided that an intruder that got this far should have the opportunity to say what they wanted to.

At five feet and eight inches tall, Joseph Stalin was relatively short for a man, and though only a fool would admit it, his time as the Soviet Premier had not been good to his frame.

He was looking out of the window, and continued to look out when the door opened.

'You are early, Dmitri,' Stalin said, turning away from the window and striding towards a drinks cabinet in the corner. Dmitri was only ever early when the matter at hand was important; it was something they had agreed upon a few years before. 'Sit down if you wish.' If there was anyone who could refuse this request it was Dmitri, but he didn't want to try his luck.

He sat in a warm red chair in front of the room's desk.

Stalin came with two tumblers and a bottle of whisky. The whisky bottle had a black label and had English writing on it.

'Where is that from?' Dmitri asked.

'Scotland,' Stalin said, filling each of the tumblers. 'Churchill sent me two cases as a gift. Churchill calls whisky "man's greatest comfort," but then he would say that, as he is rarely without a glass of it. He is a good ally, but when this war is won, doubtless we will be enemies again.'

'Surely drinking Scotch whisky goes against communism,' Dmitri said. 'Aren't we only supposed to drink Russian whisky?'

Stalin shrugged. 'If the bourgeois world can't provide Joseph Stalin and Dmitri Markov with a glass each of man's greatest comfort, what on earth is the point of the bourgeois world?'

They laughed, raised their glasses and drank their whisky in one go. Both of them set their tumblers down at the same time.

'On to the matter at hand then,' Dmitri said. Stalin sighed.

'One day you shall die, Dmitri, and then you will regret all this rushing about,' Stalin said. If it was a threat, it was very well masked.

'My apologies,' Dmitri got up to pour more whisky, 'Another glass?' he asked. Stalin shook his head.

'Nothing worse than forced conversation. Sit down and tell me what it is,' Stalin said. Dmitri sat down.

'You're to visit a children's camp tomorrow,' Dmitri began. Stalin nodded. 'I don't think you should. It's not safe.' The last sentiment reminded Stalin that Dmitri was a man he'd known his whole life; he cared about his safety.

'What if I was to promise you I will be as safe as I would be sitting in this seat?' Stalin said.

'That would be fantastic, but it would also be impossible,' Dmitri said.

'Come over here,' Stalin motioned to Dmitri to come around the table. Stalin opened a draw on his desk and took out two metal objects.

One was a small box and the other was a gun.

He pressed a button on the box and it whirred into life. Dmitri was shocked by what he saw, but kept his mouth shut. He felt like there was something more impressive to come.

Stalin fired three deafening shots and Dmitri gasped.

'How...?' Dmitri asked, astounded.

'You'd be amazed at what scientists can do when you cut them off from their families and give them a simple set of instructions,' Stalin said, enjoying the look on Dmitri's face.

Dmitri nodded slowly and walked around the table.

'How about that drink?' he asked hoarsely. Stalin smiled and nodded.

23

Cold

'That was quite a day!' exclaimed Andrea when they were back in the boys' room in the evening. 'And a pretty good meal, too!' Everyone at the camp had spent the day setting up the stage and seating for Stalin's arrival and now everyone at the camp was exhausted.

Dinner had been wonderful: a thick rich beetroot soup that the Russians called borscht, followed by baked potatoes and tasty kebabs made from a meat whose origins no one at the camp seemed to want to enquire into too closely. Some said it was beef, other sheep, some rat. Hugo didn't care; it stayed down when he swallowed it, and as far as he was concerned that was the most important thing. He wouldn't even had minded at that point if it was pork. Russia was, after all, at war and it impressed him that the camp had managed to serve such a meal at all. There was water to wash down the meal, and a weak beer which Hugo and Lottie hadn't liked but which the other three did.

Some of the other young people at the camp had tried to talk to them, but Hugo, Lottie, Andrea, Oliver and Jens had kept themselves to themselves.

'Isn't it time we phoned Germany to find out how we're getting back home?' Andrea asked.

Their plane had been shot down, and they'd been so busy taking part in the preparations for Stalin's arrival that they hadn't given much thought to returning home.

Lottie looked around at everyone, 'I'm assuming someone knows the number to call him with that radiophone thingy. They might not even know we're still alive.'

'I know the number for my uncle's house, if he's not at home one of the maids will tell me where he is,' Jens said casually.

'He has maids?' Lottie asked. Jens nodded.

'He has eleven maids and a butler that oversees everything,' Jens said. 'The butler's name's Leon Schmidt...'

'Why do we need to know his name?' Lottie asked.

'Just in case he picks up the phone,' Jens said.

'Won't you just call it?' Lottie asked him. Jens laughed and shook his head.

'There's no way I'm going to be the one that does it, my Russian won't hold up if things go wrong and I get a wrong number.'

'I'll make the call if you dial,' Hugo said, decisively.

Andrea still had the radiophone in her bag. It was only about a foot long and three inches wide, and came with an aerial that was folded into three and fitted snugly against the back of the phone to save space.

Jens dialled the number and waited nervously. After about half a minute of silence - every second that passed felt like an age to him - there was a strange beep from the radiophone and then a voice

'Yes?' the answer came in German and Hugo breathed a huge sigh of relief.

'Who am I talking to?' Hugo asked, in German.

'My name is Schmidt. I am the Goebbels family butler,' the voice said. Hugo practically jumped with excitement.

'Who am I talking to?' Schmidt demanded.

'Hugo Safin,' Hugo said quickly. 'Can I talk to Dr Goebbels?'

'Dr Goebbels is going through a particularly difficult time at the moment, so unless it's important...' Schmidt said.

'I'm a friend of his nephew, Jens,' Hugo said. 'We're on a mission together. I must talk to him.'

The change was immediate.

'Is Jens alive?' Schmidt gasped.

'Yes he's fine, but we really need to talk to Dr Goebbels,' Hugo said.

'That's excellent news!' Schmidt said. 'I'll pass you over to him immediately. Please wait a moment.'

'He's gone to get Goebbels,' Hugo said to his friends.

'Let me have a listen,' Andrea said. She walked over to Hugo's side and leaned into the radiophone.

'Hello?' came the familiar voice of the sinister Minister for Propaganda.

'Dr Goebbels!' Andrea exclaimed, far too happily for Hugo's liking.

'Andrea! Are you with Jens?' Goebbels asked. 'What happened to the plane? It never arrived. Then I found out that our eastern battlefront had moved backwards... I'm so sorry about that.' He didn't sound his usual suave self. In fact, and it pained Hugo to admit it, he sounded like a man who'd been coming to terms with the death of his nephew.

'Yes I am with Jens, and he's absolutely fine,' Andrea said. Goebbels exhaled and his voice slowed considerably.

'Thank God,' Goebbels said, 'and the plane?'

'Crash landed,' Andrea said.

'Shot down?' Goebbels asked.

'Yes,' Andrea replied.

'That must have been quite an experience to survive,' Goebbels said. Andrea looked up at Hugo. They were both thinking about a completely different thing that had happened that day.

'So where are you now? It's been eight days since you flew off,' Goebbels said.

'We're at the camp,' Andrea said.

'Oh bravo!' Goebbels said, they heard a clap in the phone. 'I'll have the details later, but that's really very impressive.'

'Minister, could you remind me where you said we were meeting those soldiers?' Hugo asked.

'Of course, give me a second,' Goebbels said. There was silence on the line, and if Hugo wasn't mistaken, he could hear the faintest sound of footsteps approaching out in the corridor. They probably weren't coming here though.

'Hurry up,' he muttered. The footsteps were getting louder.

'All right,' Goebbels said, they could hear him flattening a map out. 'It's at a town called Zaraysk, and the soldiers will arrive in two days' time. I will inform the leader of the situation, and you are to wait for them in...' Goebbels paused, probably to look down at his map.

There was a knock on the door and Hugo jumped.

'Is there anyone inside?' a boy's voice asked.

'You are to wait for them in a pub,' Goebbels said, 'called in Russian, "The Lonely Soldier", which in Russian is *Odinoki Soldat*. Zaraysk is quite a distance away, and I'm afraid that the five of you will have to make your own way there – bringing soldiers any closer to you would be too risky.'

'So let me get this straight,' Hugo said, more quietly than he had ever said anything ever before, 'two days' time, Zaraysk, the lonely soldier.'

'That's it exactly. You sound hurried, are you in a rush?' Goebbels asked.

'Just a little,' Hugo said hoarsely. He turned the phone off without another word.

'WHAT'S HAPPENING IN THERE?' the boy demanded. He knocked on the door again. 'WHY ARE YOU SPEAKING GERMAN?'

'Thank God we locked the door. Let's get the bloody hell out of here,' Hugo said.

The boy rattled the lock again. 'I SHALL GO AND FETCH A CAMP OFFICER!' the boy shouted, and they all heard his quick, heavy footsteps as he raced down the corridor outside.

'What on earth are we going to do?' Lottie asked. Hugo and Andrea both looked around the room for an opportunity to escape, and their eyes came to rest on the window at almost exactly the same time.

'We're going to jump out of the window,' they said in unison. Perhaps if they had not been in such a rush, they would have revelled in the fact that they were both thinking the same way, but this was no time for patting each other's backs. Hugo got a hold of the window frame and pushed it open as far as it could go. On the other side of the room, Jens and Andrea were dragging the bags towards the window.

'What are you doing?' Oliver asked.

'They're not going to be too willing to let us back into the camp after that boy goes and reports us. I think we should take our things with us,' Andrea said.

'Right,' Oliver said. He took the last remaining bag and hauled it to the window.

'Let's throw them out first,' Jens said.

'It'd be rather difficult to throw them out after we jump,' Lottie said.

'Not now Lottie,' Andrea said. She picked one of the bags up and pushed it out of the window. Hugo, Lottie, Andrea, Jens and Oliver listened, and there was a worryingly long period between Andrea's push and the thud of the bag onto the ground. The four other bags followed quickly afterwards, and Oliver took it upon himself to be the first to jump.

He clambered onto the frame and hopped out.

'Are you all right?' Hugo shouted down.

'I'm fine! It's quite a soft landing!' he yelled up. 'Come on you lot! Hurry!'

Hugo was next to jump, and Andrea followed him. Lottie went after Andrea and Jens jumped last.

By the time Jens landed, the rest of them had already picked a bag up and strapped it on.

'How do you know whose is whose?' Jens said, picking up the last bag.

'We don't! It'd waste too much time,' Hugo said. As Jens brought the straps of the bag over his shoulders, there was a sinking feeling in his chest. Somehow, he'd ended up with his own bag. There was really no getting away from the gun concealed inside.

As soon as Jens had his bag on his back, Hugo, Lottie, Andrea, Jens and Oliver started to run. The moon had been full less than a week earlier, and so there was still enough of it to help light their way, but not enough to make them stand out in the night. The camp's previous use as a fort meant that once they were outside the perimeter, getting away was fairly easy, especially as the guard's hut that they'd gone through on entrance was on the opposite wall to their window.

After a few minutes of aimless walking, their path crossed that of a road. They kept away from the road to avoid running into anyone, but used it as a guide. Several cars drove past as they walked and, each time, they would all drop down to their knees the second they heard the rumble of the engine.

They found a barn on the outskirts of a farm about eight kilometres from the camp. The barn was dark and smelt of cowdung as barns tend to do, but their noses soon got used to the smell, and they quickly decided its comparative warmth more than compensated for its shortcomings.

It was a big barn with plenty of room, and Hugo and Andrea walked off to find their own space in it.

'Where are you two going?' Lottie demanded.

'We just want a bit of privacy, if that's not too much to ask,' Hugo said.

Hugo and Andrea found a quiet corner of the barn, maybe thirty or so metres from Jens, Lottie and Oliver, which didn't smell quite as bad as the rest of the place. They made themselves a sort of nest of hay.

'Let's stay close together,' said Hugo.

'To conserve body heat?' Andrea asked, matter-of-factly. She was doing her utmost to remain composed, but the cold had left his voice husky and the sound of it made her toes tingle.

'Yes, body heat,' Hugo replied quickly, 'if our bodies are closer together, we'll keep each other warm.'

'That's it?' Andrea asked, though her voice was calm and soft rather than grouchy, 'is that all I am to you? A hot water bottle?'

'More or less,' Hugo said nonchalantly, 'but you're definitely one of the hotter water bottles out there,' Andrea followed the sound of his voice until she stood inches away from him.

'How hot exactly?' she asked softly.

'You're practically on fire,' Hugo said.

Kissing in near darkness is a usually a difficult thing to do, but a sixth sense told Hugo exactly where Andrea was, and he met her lips half way.

At that moment, all Hugo could really think about was how warm she was. He took a hold of her waist and she did the same. Her hair would have rendered him temporarily blind even if it hadn't been so dark there, but there is something wonderfully comforting about having a girl's hair in your face.

There was no Oliver to interrupt them, so they stayed how they were for a fair amount of time. Neither of them wanted to stop for anything as trivial as air, and, as romantic as asphyxiation via the kissing might be, they did eventually break apart to breathe.

They lay beside each other for a while and revelled in each other's company – physical affection was great, but the silence they shared was, Hugo thought, in some ways more intense, and even more exciting.

'What's it been like? Being a Jew in Nazi Germany?' Andrea asked carefully.

'Terrifying,' Hugo said. It was the first time anyone had ever asked him that, and he decided to elaborate, 'every waking moment, you're scared a Gestapo officer is going to arrest you, or that you'll say something that'll land you in trouble.'

'But surely you get used to it?' Andrea asked. Hugo shook his head instinctively, forgetting that she couldn't see his head.

'Not at all. As soon as we got used to the way things were, they got worse,' Hugo said.

'What do you mean?' Andrea asked.

'It's harder for me to say,' Hugo said, 'because the laws didn't apply to us exactly.'

'Because of your dad?' Andrea asked.

'How do you know that?' Hugo asked, giving her a quizzical look that she couldn't see. His facial expressions being useless were something that he would have to get used to.

'You said about your dad dying to keep your secret after Jens... you know,' Andrea said. 'So you're not officially a Jew?'

'I suppose I'm not,' Hugo said.

'How did your dad... you know,' Andrea asked, probing rather than asking a potentially painful question.

'A guard shot him in the base of the skull,' Hugo said, 'so at least it was quick.' Hugo rolled onto his back to look at ceiling of the barn, and Andrea did the same.

'At least he died for something,' Andrea said.

'Yeah,' Hugo said. 'What about your parents? Tell me about them, if it's all right.'

'Its fine,' Andrea said, 'my father was a journalist, one of the best in the country according to his friends. He always said he was the best though, his pride drove my brother up the wall.'

'I can imagine,' Hugo said pointedly.

'Oh whatever,' Andrea said. 'Do you want me to tell you or not?'

'Please do,' Hugo said.

'Right. Well he supported Hitler from the off. He said he was the country's saviour and that, with him in charge, we could become as strong a country as we had once been,' Andrea said guiltily.

'What did he think after Hitler showed what he would do to sort out the country?' Hugo asked. He could feel how uncomfortable she was.

'He always said that no progress worth making came without sacrifice. He saw what Hitler was doing as... necessary,' Andrea said.

'Nice man,' Hugo said.

'He was. He took really good care of us all. I remember one time...' Andrea was very slow to hear the sarcasm in Hugo's voice, 'that's my father you're talking about,' she warned.

'He sounds like he was just as bad as Jens's uncle,' Hugo said, 'as well as being arrogant.'

'Shut up,' Andrea said, her voice smouldering, 'you don't know what you're talking about.'

Hugo shrugged and there was silence.

He could feel her glare in the dark, and he did his best to project one back. The problem was his thinning resolve, and eventually, as always seemed to be the case between them, he capitulated.

'I'm sorry,' Hugo murmured reluctantly.

Andrea seemed to have been waiting for his apology, because she rolled over immediately and gave him a kiss.

'Its fine,' she said, 'I understand how hard it must be to see all of us as anything but callous monsters.'

'You're not a callous monster,' Hugo said.

'Thanks,' Andrea said with a smile, 'that really warms my heart.' Hugo laughed and gave her another kiss before rolling onto his side to fall asleep. His arm wrapped Andrea up, and brought her body close to his in a warm embrace. She'd never have admitted it to him, but his arm across her chest made her feel wonderfully secure and safe.

'You're brilliant Hugo,' she said softly, 'I don't know what I'd do if anything was to happen to you because...' she paused, struggling for a moment.

'Because you're Jewish,' she said eventually. She was silent for another while, composing herself, 'You mean the world to me, and if anything does happen, I'll be right there beside you... For better or worse.'

The implications of what she had just said shocked her – the penalties for associating with Jews, let alone loving them, could be just as horrific as the punishments for Jews themselves. The fact that she didn't doubt herself on her pledge was equally shocking, but comforting: she was with him for the long haul.

'Hugo?' Andrea asked, realising that she might have just been talking to herself. Her response was a low rumble she took as a snore, and Andrea laughed quietly to herself before making herself comfortable in Hugo's shoulder.

A quiver in Hugo's closed eyes betrayed the truth, and a solitary tear rolled down his nose.

24

Assassin

Andrea woke up before anyone else and was glad that she had – she'd fallen asleep facing Hugo, their faces inches apart, and her arms around his neck. She wouldn't have heard the end of it if they'd found her in that position.

She gave Hugo a little nudge to wake him, and he smiled blissfully at the sight of her face when he came around.

'Let's get everyone up,' Andrea said quietly. She stretched her hand down to him and he took it and got to his feet.

Hugo woke Oliver and Andrea woke Lottie. Neither of them wanted to be the one that shook Jens awake. It was the day of Stalin's visit, and it didn't seem right to remove him from whatever dream he was having.

'I'll do it if none of you will,' Oliver said, looking around at his friends. When it became clear no one else was going to volunteer, he crept over to Jens and gave him a slight push.

Jens's eyes opened the second that Oliver touched him, before he'd even nudged him.

'Are you all right?' Oliver asked. Jens got to his feet before he spoke.

'Sure,' he said.

'Did you sleep well?' Lottie asked.

'Like a baby,' Jens said sarcastically. Lottie's eyes narrowed.

'No need to be like that,' she said. 'I only asked because I was worried you hadn't slept.'

'Would you have slept?' Jens asked. 'You have no idea…'

'No I don't,' Lottie said, 'but I'm not going to listen to you complain about it for another second, this journey's hardly been a cakewalk for any of us.'

'It hasn't been anywhere near as bad for you lot as it has for me,' Jens said.

'I think Hugo would disagree,' Lottie said curtly.

'Leave me out of it,' Hugo said from behind his sister.

'Coward,' Lottie said, before returning her attention to Jens. 'You really need to come to terms with this. You'll feel bad after you've done it, but you'll get over it; especially if the war starts to turn because of it.' Jens turned from her and put his head into his hands. He went and sat on a hay bale and stared straight ahead.

'What if I can't get over it?' he asked quietly. Lottie walked towards his hay bale and sat down to his left.

'You'll have me to help you,' she said softly.

'I know that Lottie, I really do. But I feel like it's going to stay with me for the rest of my life,' Jens said.

'Then so will I,' Lottie said. She took his left hand into both of her own and he met her gaze. Lottie didn't kiss him, as if that would have ruined the moment somehow. The worry was seeping out of his gaze, and it was being replaced with a steely resolve.

All of a sudden, Hugo, Andrea and Oliver felt like they were intruding. The scene was extremely intimate, and the three of them tried to avert their eyes without making it too obvious.

'We need to decide how we're going to get to Zaraysk.' Oliver said to Hugo quietly.

'No point doing it without Jens,' Hugo replied, 'he's pretty key to the whole thing.' Jens's focus flashed away from Lottie for half a second at the sound of his name, and his eyes flickered onto Hugo.

'What was that?' he asked.

'Oh nothing,' Hugo said, 'just carry on with...'

'We need to plan what we're going to do after you've shot Stalin,' Oliver said. Lottie glared at him for being so direct but Jens didn't seem to mind.

'All right,' Jens said, standing. He smiled at Lottie and led her over to the rest of their friends.

Oliver got his bag from the barn door and retrieved his map before returning to the rest of them and kneeling down with it. He rolled it out until he found Astapova and Zaraysk on it.

'First of all, Jens, do you know where you're going to set up to take your shot?' Oliver asked. Jens thought for a second.

'I saw them preparing the platform in the camp's court-yard. You can see the whole of the courtyard from the front gates, and so I was thinking that I could...' Jens said.

'Surely you weren't thinking of taking the shot in front of the main gates?' Oliver interrupted, aghast.

'Why not?' Jens asked, 'I would go about a hundred metres back so I couldn't be seen easily from inside. The only alternative is setting up somewhere high up in the camp, which isn't too inviting an idea.'

'Fine,' Oliver said, 'if you're sure you can shoot through that distance, as well as the obstruction of the gate and guards.'

'I am,' Jens said.

'Right. Well that makes leaving the area a little easier,' Oliver said, scanning the map. 'How does hitching a ride on a train sound?' he asked.

'That wouldn't work,' Andrea said immediately.

'Why?' Oliver asked.

'The second word gets out that Stalin's been shot, the Russians are going to shut down all routes into, and out of, the area. If we were to leave quickly, then we'd have a chance of getting away before they could stop the trains, but we don't even know what time it'll go past,' Andrea said. Oliver thought about arguing with her, but it struck him that it would be unwise to go with a plan that everyone wasn't sure about.

'Why don't we drive to Zaraysk?' Lottie asked.

'Apart from the lack of a car?' Hugo asked sarcastically.

'We followed a road to get here, and we saw loads of cars,' Lottie began, 'and Jens will have a gun.'

'So we should steal a car?' Oliver said.

'Yes,' Lottie said. Jens shook his head silently, and Lottie gave him a withering look 'oh come on Jens. If it makes you feel any better we'll wait for a wealthier person to come past and we'll take theirs,'

'Fine,' Jens said humourlessly. 'What's a little theft after murder?' Oliver looked thoughtful for a second.

'And that's all right by the two of you?' Oliver asked.

'Fine by me, but who's going to drive?' Andrea asked.

'My parents let me drive from one end of our road to the other a few times when I visited them last,' Oliver said. 'I'll be able to figure it out.'

Hugo and Andrea looked at each other, silently convening, before they both nodded.

'That's settled then,' Oliver said. 'Jens, I think you ought to walk back to the camp now. We'll wait here for you. Do you remember the way or will you need the map?'

'I'll be all right,' he said.

'Do you want me to come with you?' Lottie asked.

'No!' Jens said immediately. 'No, there's no way you're going anywhere near that dreadful place again!' Lottie was taken aback by his tenacity and she didn't press the issue.

Jens walked over to the bags, found his and checked its contents, then slung it over his shoulder. Then he moved towards the barn door and pulled it open.

'Back in a jiffy,' he said over his shoulder, and he let the door close behind him.

To Jens's disappointment, the walk to the camp didn't take long at all. He stopped his normal walk as soon as the fort was in sight, and he crouched down and began to move in a covert manner. His white coat camouflaged him well against the snowy landscape.

When he was about a hundred metres away from the camp's gate, he went flat onto his chest and dug around in his bag. He produced the telescopic sight; he would soon attach to the top of his gun, and looked into the camp's courtyard.

The courtyard was transformed, with flags and regalia all around the perimeter and a stage at the far end of the space. The stage stretched from one side of the square to the other, and there was a red curtain adorned with the the hammer and sickle hiding the people behind it.

The young pioneers had just started to filter into the courtyard, and once the first row had assembled, Jens took his eye away from the sight and began to take the rest of the pieces of the gun out of his bag.

It was relatively simple to put together, and there was a clip of five bullets at the very bottom of his bag.

Jens got himself comfortable and pushed the clip into the gun, pulling back the small handle on it to load a bullet into the breech.

When he looked through the telescopic sight, which was now firmly attached to the top of the gun, he realised he'd made a massive mistake.

The holes between the metal of the fort's gate were about the same size as two of Jens's palms beside each other, so he would have to shoot the bullet through one of these holes as well as hitting Stalin from about two hundred metres away.

It was more of a trick shot than anything else, and Jens did his best to forget what would happen if he missed. It was too late to change his plan now, Stalin would be here soon.

The assembled young pioneers were talking to each other excitedly, but a ripple went through the curtain and the children fell silent instantly.

Stalin was not the first person to emerge. First out was a bald man, with a stern expression, who looked to Hugo to be about two metres tall. The next person's face was completely different, milder in its expression, but both their bodies were equally large and intimidating.

Ten more men of similar build emerged before Stalin made his appearance. He stood what looked like a foot below the shortest of the assembled men, but they parted to let him walk by.

Jens expected him to walk to the front, to the very edge of the stage, but he stopped halfway through his tunnel of men and they formed a circle around him. A curse slipped Jens's lips. He could only see strips of the man!

Stalin now had a further six thickly built men on either side of him, which did nothing to make the shot harder, but made Jens a little more wary. He didn't want to hit a guard by mistake. He would give himself away before the job was done.

The Soviet leader looked over the children in front of him, smiling and catching a few of their gazes for fleeting moments before moving on.

Jens took a moment to pick his hole in the gate and train the sight on Stalin before allowing his finger to close around the trigger. As soon as Stalin opened his smiling mouth to speak, Jens flexed his index finger and fired.

Two things happened as soon as the bullet cracked out of the gun and hit Stalin in the forehead. The dictator stumbled, and before Jens could see him fall completely, his guard enveloped him to shield him from further bullets.

There was panic in the courtyard, but Jens had no time to admire the accuracy of his shot. He had to move. Fast.

He got up off his chest and back into a crouched position, before quickly picking the gun up and moving away from the fort.

As soon as the fort began to fade from vision, he stood up straight and began to run.

'I hope Jens is all right,' Lottie said. She was resting her head on her brother's shoulder, something she hadn't done for years.

'He'll be fine,' Hugo said. 'You saw that tree back at War School. There's no way he's going to miss,'

'That's not what I'm worried about,' Lottie said. 'He might not be able to cope with it. And he's got a gun…'

'Don't even think about that Lottie,' Andrea had said from the door. She was keeping a lookout with Oliver.

'It's all I've been able to think about,' Lottie admitted sadly.

'Don't worry,' Hugo said, 'there's no way that he would…'

'There's a car coming!' Oliver shouted into the barn. 'I can't see who's driving it though!'

The car pulled up to the door, and the driver threw the door open. It was Jens, and his right hand was still clenched around the brown gun. He was wearing his YPOSU uniform and he looked cold.

'Come on then,' Jens said. Oliver was shocked at the sound of his voice. There was no emotion in it at all.

Oliver stuck his head inside and shouted at the rest of them.

'It's Jens! He's got a car! Come on!'

Lottie got off her brother's shoulder immediately and rushed to get her bag before practically sprinting to the door. Hugo, Andrea and Oliver followed her lead, although in a slightly less frantic manner.

Lottie hugged Jens as tightly as she could, but it was almost like hugging stone. Jens put his arms around her, but there was no warmth in them.

'Jens you're freezing,' Lottie said, putting his lack of feeling down to him being cold. 'Where's your coat?'

'I gave it to the man I stole the car from, as well as the rest of my money' Lottie took a step back from him. He sounded so shattered and flat it almost broke her heart.

Oliver led the rest of them out of the barn, and sat in the driver's seat of the car.

'Lottie,' Oliver said apologetically. 'We have to go. Soon they're going to start closing off the area, if they haven't already.' She nodded once and helped Jens into the middle of the back seat. Andrea sat in the front passenger seat, with Lottie and Hugo on either side of Jens.

Jens hadn't turned the engine off, and so Oliver didn't even have to start the car. He reversed the car back onto the road, before doing one final gear-change and driving off.

PART THREE:

Consequences

25

Brooding

As they drove, it became very clear that Jens was not coping with what he'd done at all. He answered questions with the least amount of words he could, and there was often a long wait before anything said to him registered.

There was an air of guilt as well. They had pressured him into doing it. Hugo realised Jens was in shock, and they would have to wait until later to hear what happened. Nobody else asked any more questions either. They must've thought the same.

They arrived in Zaraysk a few moments after nightfall, amazed that they'd arrived there without a hitch. It was a small town, the kind of place that's rife with family feuds and where outsiders are made to feel as such.

The Lonely Soldier wasn't hard to find. It was the only place in the town with its lights on, and while the town promised intrusive questions and suspicion, the pub looked warm and inviting.

They strode in, and Hugo paid for three rooms using the rest of their money. The old man at the desk looked like he wanted to ask them a million questions, but he held his tongue and took them up to their rooms in silence

None of them were surprised when Jens asked to sleep by himself.

26

Bernard

Hugo was the first to wake up in the morning, and a glance at his room's clock told him it was half past eight. He rushed to Oliver's bed, and rocked him until he woke up.

'What do you want?' he asked groggily, in Russian.

'I want you to get up,' Hugo said, also in Russian. He left the room and knocked on the door of the room Lottie was sharing with Andrea.

'Who is it?' Andrea asked in Russian.

'Hugo,' he said. 'I don't know what time we're being picked up, so I think we should be downstairs as early as possible.' There was a quiet groan, and muffled sounds of laborious movement, before Lottie and Andrea came out of their room, looking irritated and half-asleep.

'Should I wake up Jens?' Lottie asked.

'Already up,' Jens said from behind his open door. He closed it behind him as he joined them.

'Sleep well?' Lottie asked, looking for some sign of life in his flat eyes.

'Not terribly,' Jens said. It would be easy to dismiss his brevity as unfamiliarity with Russian, but they were all fairly sure he would be as abrupt with them whatever language he was speaking.

'Downstairs then,' Hugo said. Hugo, Lottie, Andrea, Jens and Oliver plodded down the stairs in single file, before choosing a round table in the pub and sitting around it.

A woman sat at the bar crying. She had several empty mugs to her left, and one to her right half full of a golden liquid. Moved, Hugo got up to talk to her. The company of a crying woman seemed to him infinitely better than Jens's company at the moment.

'What's wrong?' he asked her, sitting in the stool to her right. She looked up at Hugo, her eyes unfocused and watery.

'How can you ask me that? Yesterday...' she began. Hugo knew what was coming, but he didn't stop her, 'our leader was assassinated,' she hissed the last word, and it seemed to hang in the air for several seconds after her mouth had closed.

Hugo was lucky the woman wasn't sober enough to notice the delay in his reaction; his hands covered his mouth in shock.

'Surely not,' he said, perhaps overdoing his surprise a little. The woman got to her feet, and wobbled around the bar toward a small radio. She flicked it on.

The Russian was too quick and too static-infused for Hugo to get more than the gist of what was being said.

There were several mentions of the shooting, Astapova a few times, and every second word seemed to be 'traitors' or 'revenge'.

The woman flicked the radio off.

'Do you see now?' she asked. Hugo nodded and the woman went back to her drink, messily refilling one of her old mugs from a tap behind the bar.

Hugo was about to return to his table, when the doors of the pub crashed open.

Three distinctly un-Russian men walked into the pub. They might not have been in uniform, but it was obvious they were soldiers. One of them looked very familiar. Hugo guessed he must have been a recent graduate of War School.

The familiar looking one took a scrap of paper from his pocket.

'We're looking for Jens G...,' his eyes widened, Jens's surname wasn't one that would go unnoticed so he didn't finish it. Jens got to his feet and the rest of them did the same.

'Please follow us,' one of the other soldiers said. Hugo was only too happy to oblige. The soldier that was yet to say anything tipped his hat to the woman, who looked to be on the verge of passing out.

Once the doors closed behind them, and they had put enough distance between themselves and the pub to take them out of earshot, Andrea ran up to the familiar looking soldier and jumped into his arms.

'Bernie!' she yelped happily.

'It's been far too long,' the soldier said, cradling Andrea as if she were a baby. Hugo allowed them to stare into each other's eyes contentedly for a good ten seconds before he coughed.

'Who are you?' he asked. Andrea looked from Hugo's unwittingly menacing expression to the man she had called Bernie and started laughing.

'Calm down, Hugo,' she said with a smile, 'this is my brother,' Hugo mellowed immediately, and Bernie started to laugh as well. He put his sister down and stuck out a hand for Hugo to shake.

'Captain Bernard Ducasse, currently of the Third Panzer Army and the Brandenburgers special forces unit,' he said. Hugo took his hand.

'Hugo Safin,' he said. He felt a bit useless, not having something that he could tag onto the end of his name.

Bernard went around them all, giving his name and rank in a slightly different way every time. He didn't miss the lack of life in Jens's eyes.

'Come on then,' Bernard said, walking to a green truck, not dissimilar to the black ones they had seen a few days before.

The other two Brandenburgers got into the front seats of the truck, leaving Bernard to sit with his sister and their friends in the covered trailer.

'Are we driving back to Germany?' Oliver asked. Bernard shook his head.

'Just to German-controlled Russia, we'll get a plane from there back to Germany,' Bernard said.

They all settled into the sides of the truck, preparing to catch up on the sleep that Hugo had taken away from them earlier.

It took a lot longer to get back to German-controlled Russia than they had expected. They had still not arrived when the sky started to darken.

Jens sat in a corner. He looked down through a hole in the bottom of the truck's floor and he could see the ground fly past.

The rest of them were asleep, and not for the first time he considered jumping out of the truck.

'So are you the one that did it?' It was Bernard. It occurred to Jens that Andrea's brother could well have been watching him for hours. Jens didn't have the energy to be coy.

'Yeah,' Jens said. Bernard nodded sadly.

'You shot Stalin?' he asked. Jens's friends had avoided talking about it so explicitly, but Bernard didn't beat around the bush at all.

'Yeah,' Jens said again.

'Difficult shot?' Bernard asked, perhaps hoping for a different word.

'I didn't miss,' Jens said. He didn't say it arrogantly, he almost sighed the words out of his mouth.

'Really?' Bernard said, smiling a little. Jens remained stony faced. There was a short silence. Bernard opened his mouth to speak, but Jens got there first.

'I don't want to be preached to about what's right and what's wrong. I've had plenty of time to think about it.' It was the longest thing Jens had said for almost two days; the sensation of talking was unfamiliar.

'Then I won't preach to you,' Bernard said. 'I have a question for you.'

'Fire away,' Jens said with a humourless laugh.

'I'm assuming, because this has hit you so hard, you think Stalin's life was worth the same as everyone else's,' Bernard said.

'Go on,' Jens replied, trying to curtail his interest.

'You're right,' Bernard said. Jens couldn't hide his surprise. Bernard continued, 'but, if every life is worth the same, how many lives has Stalin extinguished?' he asked. 'Go on, take a guess.'

'I don't know. A hundred thousand?' Jens suggested.

'Eight hundred thousand, and that's just Germans,' Bernard said. 'And he was on course to kill at least that many more,' he added.

'It's still not a good thing to do,' Jens said.

'Jesus Christ, Jens,' Bernard said, 'good and bad are irrelevant! We're talking about right and wrong, and taking one life to save another eight hundred thousand, mostly innocent lives, is definitely right,' Bernard said. 'If you were looking for goodness, you should never have come in the first place.'

'I didn't have a choice,' Jens said.

'Granted, but the good thing is quite often not necessarily the right thing. You'll see that more and more as you get older,' Bernard said.

'I didn't want to come at all actually,' Jens said. Bernard shrugged.

'You've got to make the best of bad situations,' he said. Jens's eyes flicked to Lottie, and then to Hugo.

'What about what's happening to the Jews? Is that right or good?' he asked. He was fully expecting Bernard to back-track or to say that the situation with the Jews was different, but Bernard, who couldn't be more than twenty-five, leaned against the wall of the truck and sighed the sigh of a man four times his age.

'Sometimes,' Bernard began, staring straight into Jens's eyes, 'sometimes making the best of a bad situation is still one of the worst things imaginable.'

27

Praise

Adolf von Ribbentrop's office at War School seemed to Hugo nowhere near as intimidating as it had been the first time around. Hugo sat with Oliver and Andrea to his right; and Jens and Lottie on his left, all five of them with their SS uniform, smarter than it had ever been before.

Before returning to War School, Andrea, Oliver and Jens had all privately promised to Hugo and Lottie not to reveal to anyone about them being Jewish.

Lottie's collar had three bars on it, and she was furious that the judging panel had not found her seventy-two hour masterpiece worthy of first place. Hugo had been given his second bar and Oliver had been brought up to two-bars, with the promise of more to come in the near future.

As well as their ranking bars, each of them had a golden bar with a small S engraved on it. The S stood for Stalin and, seeing this, the other students at War School treated Hugo, Lottie, Andrea, Jens and Oliver with reverence. Being admired was a new feeling for all of them excluding perhaps Andrea, and they were thoroughly enjoying the experience.

They were not here to see the director though; they were waiting for Jens's uncle.

Dr Goebbels came in suddenly and quickly, and he was accompanied by someone Hugo had never imagined seeing with him: His mother.

She waved at her children, and Lottie and Hugo gave confused waves back.

Dr Goebbels strode ahead and took his seat behind the desk. Andrea guessed at her identity and offered Anna her chair, but she shook her head.

'I'll be fine standing,' she said. It was a joy for Hugo and Lottie to hear their mother's voice after two months.

'Are you sure, Anna? I could have a chair brought over,' Goebbels said. Hugo wasn't sure how to take the fact that his mother was on first name terms with Joseph Goebbels.

'I'll be fine, Joseph,' she said.

'Of course, if you're all right,' Goebbels said. He turned to face the children, 'now, what on earth has been going on?'

Goebbels' expression was frozen in awe for a solid twenty minutes as Andrea recounted their journey. She glossed over a few of the more sordid details, but Anna, who was watching her carefully, seemed to have a pretty good idea of what had happened between four of them

When Andrea finished, Goebbels' face went back to normal, and the chief Nazi propagandist made a bridge on the desk with his fingers.

'If it wasn't for the reports our spies have been bringing us out of Russia that back up everything you've said, I'd be inclined to think you were lying to me,' he said eventually.

'Every word of it is the truth,' Andrea said. Goebbels nodded.

'Of course,' he said. 'Now there is the issue of your reward. I had planned a medal ceremony already, but after hearing what has happened; I think greater decorations are in order.'

'Pardon?' Andrea said.

'Decorations are just medals and awards,' Goebbels said sagely.

'I think she was asking if we're seriously going to be given medals,' Jens said. For whatever reason, Jens's mood had been improving since they'd left Bernard's truck.

'You most certainly are,' Goebbels said resolutely, 'Germany is good to its heroes,' Hugo did feel rather good after that compliment, but as usual with Goebbels, the thought of what would happen if he knew their secret kept his happiness in check.

'When is this decoration meant to take place?' Oliver asked.

'The day after tomorrow in Freiburg,' Goebbels said.

'Why Freiburg?' Anna asked. Hugo looked at his mother, and saw the strangest thing. The slight narrowing of her eyes and the even slighter furrowing of her brow told him she was thinking, quickly and intensely. Why she would be was a mystery to Hugo, but he was sure beyond any doubt that she was.

'You are aware of Freiburg's location I'm sure,' Goebbels said. Anna nodded. 'Recently, a few men and women have attempted to leave the German Reich into Switzerland from there. They think the war has turned against us.'

Everyone in the room but Anna knew this to be the truth, but Goebbels didn't go into it.

'So the ceremony is being held there to boost morale and stop people from leaving?' Lottie said. Goebbels looked taken aback and nodded, before leaning towards his nephew.

'Make sure you keep a hold of this one,' he said to his nephew sagely. They both went red and Anna laughed. 'Yes Lottie, that's correct. I think a ceremony celebrating the death of the Reich's greatest enemy, besides Roosevelt, would be a fantastic boost to morale.' Goebbels picked up a stack of papers and flicked through them. 'A car will be sent to your house in the morning.'

'I'd prefer to drive them myself,' Anna said. 'I haven't seen them in a long time, and it would be a wonderful opportunity to talk.'

Goebbels shrugged.

'Whatever you'd like. I'll have documents drawn up that'll get you through the state borders without any hassle,' he said. 'See you in two days.' They all shook Goebbels' hand and left the director's office.

'Would you like to stay the night at our house?' Anna asked Andrea, Oliver and Jens, 'then we could leave together in the morning?' The three of them nodded enthusiastically.

'If it's not too much trouble,' Oliver said.

'No trouble at all,' Anna said. 'If the three of you get some overnight clothes and meet us here, we can be off within the hour.'

Andrea, Jens and Oliver walked towards War School's courtyard and left Anna alone with Hugo and Lottie.

'It's great to see you, Mother,' Lottie said. Anna shot a wary glance at the receptionist that was sitting outside the director's office before she replied.

'It's good to see you too,' she said with a hasty smile.

'What's wrong?' Hugo asked. His mother shook her head once.

'Not here, come.' She led Hugo and Lottie out of War School's front doors and took them a good few paces away from the building before she elaborated, 'We are escaping to Switzerland.'

Hugo and Lottie were a lot more surprised than scared. They glanced at each other and then at their mother, who looked distinctly uncomfortable.

'Why do we need to do that?' Hugo asked. 'We aren't even legally Jewish.'

'The Reichstag has passed a bill that means people suspected of being traitors can be imprisoned without a trial,' Anna said. 'Holzmann's coming for us.'

'That doesn't make any sense,' Hugo said. Anna sighed impatiently.

'Nothing has made any sense for the past eight years,' she said.

'We can't just leave,' Lottie said. 'Isn't there any other way we could...'

'Not unless you want to go into hiding, which is risky at best,' Anna replied. 'Look Lottie, I know you've made friends here, but they don't know the truth about us. What do you think Jens would think if he knew?' Lottie bit her lip to stop herself from replying.

'Where will we stay?' Hugo asked.

'With your father's parents. I've sent a letter,' Anna said. Hugo nodded. The three of them stood in silence, looking at anything but each other.

'Can we at least tell our friends we're leaving?' Lottie asked.

'Absolutely not,' Anna said. 'The less they know about this the better.' Lottie looked like she was about to protest, but Anna shook her head and pointed at War School's doors.

Jens, Andrea and Oliver came out holding small bags and wearing grins on their faces.

'Got everything?' Anna asked.

'I think so,' Andrea said.

'Let's go then,' Anna said.

28

A new direction

Andrea was suspicious.

Hugo had been strangely distant at his house, barely talking to her through the night and refusing to meet her gaze in the morning.

She was sitting next to him in the back seat of Anna's car, but she might as well have been on the side of the road. Andrea had become used to his attention, and not having it was both eye opening and infuriating.

From what she could see, Lottie was behaving much the same way that her brother was. She was reading a book and Andrea hadn't seen her look up once.

'Have any of you been to Freiburg before?' Oliver asked. There was silence until Anna decided to try to start a sort of distraction.

'No I haven't, Oliver, have you?' she asked.

'Once, with War School. There's a huge botanical garden,' Oliver said.

'I didn't know you liked plants,' Anna said, losing interest in what they were talking about by the second. Oliver shrugged.

'It's all science, I guess,' he said. Anna nodded and turned her attention back to the road.

Oliver wished he had something to occupy his attention. The car was a horrible place to be with none of his friends talking, and he felt like he was outside everything that was going on, looking in.

The feeling of fifth wheel was not one that Oliver was unused to, but he hated it all the same. In Russia, he'd at least had the role of navigator, something he brought to the other four. But here, he felt worse than useless.

'Anna, how long until we arrive in Freiburg?' Oliver asked.

'Quite a while,' she said, 'Freiburg's quite a distance away from Hamburg,' Oliver groaned inwardly and tried to get some sleep.

Oliver did eventually manage to fall asleep and thankfully, he opened his eyes just as they passed the Freiburg city limits.

The hotel that Goebbels had sent them details of was hardly difficult to find, it took the most prominent position in the city centre, rivalling the adjacent town hall for splendour. The Hotel seemed to have been converted from a different type of building completely, but Oliver couldn't decide whether it had been a cathedral or a government building of some sort.

They parked in front of the hotel, and all five children got out as quickly as they could in an attempt to leave the car's sombre atmosphere behind.

Anna opened up the boot of the car to remove their bags.

Hugo's bag came out first, and Andrea was surprised to see how big it was. It was easily five times larger than hers was.

'Oh,' she said. His near silence suddenly made sense, as did his reluctance to look at her.

'What?' Anna asked, her eyes narrowed slightly.

'Nothing,' Andrea said. She stole a glance at Jens, who looked to have realised something similar. Anna still looked suspicious when they were walking up to the Hotel, but

Andrea didn't pay her any attention. She was making a decision.

Anna went to the front desk, and started to talk to the receptionist. Andrea put her bags down in the lobby.

'Jens, could I talk to you for a moment?' Andrea asked him.

'Sure,' Jens said. He stayed where he was standing.

'In private,' she said.

'Oh, OK,' Jens put his bags down and followed Andrea back out into the road. She looked over her shoulder several times to make sure that no one was following them before she began to speak.

'You know what's happening right?' she asked. Jens nodded.

'They're leaving,' he said, 'I don't know why, but it's obvious.'

'I know,' Andrea said, 'but that's not what I wanted to talk to you about.'

'Go on,' Jens said.

'I wanted to know what you were going to do,' Andrea said. Jens looked out onto the road and scratched his chin.

'I have no idea,' he said, 'I mean, of course I want to go, but you know who my uncle is. He might convince the government to issue a search warrant. It could put them in more danger.' The way he said it made it sound like something that had been done before. 'What are you going to do?'

'I think I'll go with them, if I can convince Anna to let me come,' Andrea said. 'I don't want to leave Hugo. I love him. I can always write Bernie a letter. Also, I have a horrible feeling that the war is going to go very badly for Germany, and frankly I'd rather not be around when that happens.'

'I'm a little torn about whether to go if you ask me,' Andrea turned around to see Oliver's green eyes staring at her. He didn't look especially angry, rather his face was relaxed in a way that promised yelling if they weren't tactful.

'Oliver... I didn't see you come out,' Jens said.

'That was the point,' Oliver said shortly.

'Are you going to try and come?' Andrea asked.

'Come? Surely you mean go? I'm fairly sure Anna's going to be against you going with them,' Oliver said. He didn't sound sour, he was simply stating facts, 'and do you have any idea where they're going? They could be on their way back to Russia, although I'd say France is a lot more likely.'

'You didn't answer my question,' was all Andrea said.

'I don't know. If you all treat me the same way that you do here, I'm not sure if I want to,' Oliver said.

'How do we treat you?' Jens asked. Oliver was determined not to sound pitiful. He stood up straight and looked Jens in the eye.

'You treat me like a fifth wheel,' he said. Andrea held back the sympathetic coo that she wanted to give, because she knew how much it would irritate him.

'That's possibly true,' Jens said, 'and I'm sorry about it. You shouldn't think that we don't value you though. You're our friend and we'd definitely miss you if you weren't there.'

'Yeah, and we'd never have survived in Russia without you,' Andrea added.

'That's nice of you to say, but...' Oliver began.

'But nothing,' Andrea said sharply. 'We're all going with the Safins.' Andrea led the two boys back into the hotel where Anna was waiting.

'You three are in a room together,' she said, 'but we're all on the twelfth floor,' Jens, Andrea and Oliver picked their bags back up and followed Anna up the hotel's stairs.

'Who's going to ask?' Jens whispered. He was standing outside the Safins' room with Andrea and Oliver.

'I'll do it,' Oliver said, his voice barely audible.

'OK,' Jens said, 'whenever you're ready.' Oliver took a deep breath and knocked on the door.

'Hello?' it was Lottie.

'Could we come in?' Oliver asked.

'Of course,' Lottie said. 'The door should be open.' Oliver twisted the doorknob and the three of them came in.

Anna was sitting on the corner of her bed with Hugo. Lottie was lying on the floor, sketching something.

'Hello, Oliver?' Anna said. She was very obviously asking what he was doing in their room, but as politely as she could.

'We wanted to ask you a few things,' Oliver said.

'Go right ahead,' Anna said, slightly less enthusiastically.

'We wanted to know why you were leaving, where you were going, and if we could come as well,' Oliver said, counting the three things off on his fingers.

'We aren't going anywhere,' Anna said. 'Where on earth have you got that idea from?'

'Your bags are far too big for two nights away,' Oliver pointed out. Anna chose to ignore him.

'Why would we want to leave our country?' Anna asked. 'Just as we stand on the brink of controlling the entire continent...' Lottie obviously hadn't inherited her ability to lie from her father.

'You're Jews, though,' Andrea said quietly. Anna certainly hadn't expected that, and the shock in her expression gave her away.

'Lottie, Hugo?' Anna said. Her two children looked at their mother, who was now angrier than they had ever seen her.

'Yes, Mother?' they asked, pretty much in unison.

'How do they know we're Jewish?' Anna asked calmly.

'We told them,' Hugo said sheepishly, 'but they more or less figured it out before we admitted it,' he added.

'You are aware, aren't you, that your father died – died – to keep our religion a secret!' Anna exclaimed. 'He gave his LIFE to stop anyone finding out what you've been telling everyone about!' Anna said.

'It wasn't like that!' Lottie shouted. 'We only told three people!'

'One of whom is a relative of one of the most evil men in the world,' Anna retorted, 'how could you know they wouldn't tell anyone?'

'We would never...' Andrea said, horrified by the thought. Anna looked straight at her, and she was surprised by how appalled Andrea actually was.

'Not in a million years,' Jens said confidently.

'You said you wanted to come with us,' Anna said with a glance at Andrea. 'What about your parents?'

'Not a problem,' Andrea said. 'They died in a mountaineering accident.'

'I'm very sorry to hear that,' Anna said. 'I'm very sorry indeed.'

She glanced at Jens. 'What about you Jens?' Anna asked. 'I know enough about your uncle to guess his reaction, but what about your mother and father? I'm sure they'll be worried,' Anna said.

'I can't continue to live in a country and in a house that thinks of people as wonderful as you all as scum,' Jens said. 'It's not right.'

'Thank you, Jens,' Anna said. 'It's... it's very good of you to say that. And truly enlightened of you, too. But your parents will be worried, won't they? You're their son, after all.'

'I'll write them a letter after we're there then. Just so they know I'm safe,' Jens said. Anna seemed satisfied by this.

'And you, Oliver?' Anna asked.

'My parents were thinking of buying a house in Latvia,' he said. 'They like doing that, being the first Germans to buy property in newly conquered territory.' Anna looked at him as if she were expecting him to start laughing, but his face stayed straight. 'I'll just write them a letter,' he added.

'You must be pretty well off for them to have a hobby like that,' Lottie said. Oliver shrugged.

'It keeps them busy,' he said.

'Right,' Anna said, 'well, I think it would be best if we leave after the ceremony tomorrow. And I'm telling you now, one of the first things I'm going to do in Switzerland is enrol you all in a school. There's no way you're getting out of education that easily.'

'Switzerland,' Jens said, letting the word roll on his tongue, 'I've never been there.'

'I don't suppose you have,' Anna said. 'My late husband's parents have lived there for the best part of a decade.'

'Is their house big enough?' Andrea asked.

'Easily. They have more than enough space,' Anna said. She clapped her hands suddenly and got to her feet. 'Now, I have a letter to write to my father-in-law. You three had better be ready to travel as soon as the ceremony is finished tomorrow. You'll have to leave everything else you own behind.'

Jens, Oliver and Andrea nodded and left the room. Now that the problem had been solved, conversation flowed between them like wine at a wedding, and all was well.

29

Breaking and Entering

Holzmann wore a triumphant smile on his unpleasant face as he strode towards his car. Clenched in his right hand was a document that he had dreamt about for months: an arrest warrant for the Safins. He opened it out to read it again, but his eyes skipped down the paper to the small clause at the bottom, which said he could 'use necessary force' to bring them in.

He had a gun strapped to his waist, hidden underneath his jacket; and he intended to use it if the Safins were anything but docile and pleading.

Holzmann took the scenic route to the Safin's house, driving past several acres of open moor and private land. He took every inch of the beautiful German countryside in, eagerly anticipating the day that it would be completely free of scum.

His first pang of uncertainty came when he saw their drive. It was empty.

He calmed himself with the knowledge that they couldn't possibly have known he was coming. He got out of his car and walked imperiously towards the house, stopping at the door and rapping it three times with his knuckles.

'Open the door!' he shouted. There was no urgency in his voice the first time, but the fourth time he shouted it, his voice broke and he was suddenly angry. Holzmann prepared to ram the door open, but after taking a few paces out he remembered his gun.

He pulled the hammer, took aim, and shot the lock.

The door exploded open with the enormous force of the round, and Holzmann rushed inside, listening out for any sounds of movement that weren't his own.

He began his search with an enthusiastic savagery, like a shark in bloody water. He rushed into room after room, barging the doors open and sometimes firing a few bullets inside. Eventually, after his second round of searching, he came to the conclusion that the Safins had vacated their house.

He ran down the house's stairs and into the kitchen. There were a frantic few seconds of searching before he found the telephone, and he dialled the number for his Gauleiter. The Gauleiter, Heinrich Schlimm, was the most powerful man in the province, and Holzmann took great pride in the fact that he was only one rank below him. If there was anyone capable of finding out where the Safins had gone, assuming they hadn't gone into hiding, it was him.

The phone rang twice before it was picked up.

'This is the Gauleiter's office. Please state your name and business,' the secretary said.

'Gustav Holzmann,' Holzmann said. He didn't need to state his business; the secretary knew exactly who he was.

'One moment,' there was some clicking and the sound of movement on the other side of the phone before the line was graced with a new voice.

'Holzmann!' the man's tone was friendly and familiar, 'what can I do for you?'

'I'm looking for a family of traitors,' Holzmann said, 'their house is empty and I'm holding a warrant for their arrest.'

'Happy hunting!' the man said jovially. 'What's the surname?' he asked.

'Safin,' Holzmann said. 'There's a mother and two children; a son and a daughter.'

'Can't say the name rings a bell,' the man said. 'I'll call around and see what I can find.'

'Thank you, Herr Schlimm,' Holzmann said.

'Any time,' he said. 'I'll call you back on this number in a couple hours.' Schlimm hung up, leaving Holzmann to listen to static for a few seconds before he did the same.

Holzmann now found himself in a strange situation. He was inside the Safin's house with two hours to kill. First things first, he decided, rolling up his sleeves, he was going to make breakfast.

Two hours later, and Holzmann had filled himself with the Safin's food. The house's pantry was surprisingly well stocked, and he'd had himself a veritable feast.

Holzmann was just getting himself comfortable when the phone began to ring. He got up quickly and rushed back into the kitchen and picked up the phone but he waited for the person on the other end to speak first. He couldn't be sure that it was Schlimm.

'Holzmann?' He let out a sigh of relief. It was Schlimm all right.

'I'm here,' Holzmann said, 'what have you got for me?'

'You're not going to believe this,' Schlimm began, 'but later today, they're going to be given the Order of the German Cross for significantly aiding the war effort.'

'Pardon?' Holzmann asked. 'What have they done to deserve it?'

'No idea,' Schlimm said. 'It's all very top secret, but the person that informed me said there was going to be a public announcement at some point in the next week.'

'And who was that?' Holzmann asked, preparing to discredit the cretin that had informed his boss.

'Joseph Goebbels,' Schlimm said. Holzmann almost dropped the receiver in surprise, 'and he also asked me to give you a warning.'

'What did he say?' Holzmann asked.

'He said that the Safins are national heroes, and any inquest against them would be met with significant political weight.' Schlimm said. Holzmann's hand had drifted down to his gun, and he was gripping the handle tightly.

'You didn't give him my name, did you?' Holzmann asked, trying to sound blasé and unconcerned.

'No,' Schlimm said. 'Why, you aren't thinking of going after them are you?' he asked.

Holzmann was silent for a moment too long. 'No, I'm just interested,' he said, 'I don't suppose he told you when and where the decoration ceremony is being held?' Schlimm sighed.

'It's being held in Freiburg, in about six hours,' Schlimm said.

'Right,' Holzmann replied.

'Just watch what you do. I won't stand against Goebbels to defend you,' Schlimm said warily. Holzmann put down the receiver.

Hamburg to Freiburg was usually a seven-hour journey, he thought, picking his jacket from a chair and pulling it on.

He'd have to do it faster.

30

The Chase

It had been surprisingly easy for the Safins and their friends to make their way away from the awards ceremony. Goebbels had made a short speech, and then Hugo, Lottie, Andrea, Jens and Oliver had been given their medals.

Goebbels had seemed especially proud as he fixed the medal to his nephew's chest, but Jens looked away from him, perhaps regretting the decision he'd made a little.

The applause went on for just as long as was polite considering the occasion, but no longer. The assembled Nazi bureaucrats and obscure politicians looked like they couldn't wait to leave the ceremony.

'I'm going to Italy for a few weeks,' Goebbels had said to Jens, 'so you might not hear from me for a bit.'

'See you whenever then,' Jens had said, hugging his uncle. Goebbels was the last of the audience to leave, so the six of them found themselves standing in Freiburg Plaza, completely alone.

They walked to Anna's car and got inside. The plan had been to make their way away from the plaza quickly, but the lack of onlookers meant that they dawdled a little.

Freiburg was a pretty little city, and it was all the more beautiful in the afternoon, when people were making their way home from work and picking up children. The people of Freiburg gave the place life.

Eventually, Anna drove out of the city and towards the Swiss border.

It was impossible for the team to not feel elated, especially Hugo and Lottie.

'What's your grandparents' house in Switzerland like?' Oliver asked.

'We've never been,' Hugo said.

'Mrs Safin?' Oliver asked, redirecting his question.

'It's very spacious,' Anna said. 'It looks a little like War School on the outside, but smaller, obviously.'

'It sounds great,' Oliver said sincerely.

'There's a lake a few minutes' walk away, if my memory serves me,' Anna said. Oliver tried to imagine the place that Anna described and an involuntary smile spread across his face.

Oliver rested his head on the window, looking out at the south German landscape. The falling sun produced beautiful shadows from the trees and small houses that they drove past, and for the first time since deciding to come, he thought about the country that he was saying goodbye to. Despite its problems, Germany was his homeland, he loved her, and he didn't know when he would see her again.

Oliver was just nodding off when the rear window shattered.

'What on earth was that?' Anna asked, turning around to look at the smashed window. Silence. Memories of the side of the plane ripping off stirred in the children as cold air suddenly filled the car.

'Probably a loose stone or something,' Andrea eventually said, 'that happens sometimes doesn't it?'

'Not really,' Anna said, but she continued to drive all the same.

A few seconds later, Oliver felt something whistle past his head and the front window went the same way as the rear one. Anna shielded her eyes to protect them from glass; and when she looked back at the road, she came dangerously close to driving off it.

'I think someone's shooting at us,' Oliver shouted. The wind rushing through both of the broken windows trailed their hair behind their heads and made it difficult to be heard without shouting, but they got the gist of what Oliver had said and they ducked down. It wasn't the first time they'd been shot at.

'Why on earth would anyone be shooting at us?' Andrea asked.

'Can you see what car it is?' Anna yelled back. She didn't know why she was asking; there was only one person who would be obsessed enough to chase and shoot at them. She sped up, driving at a speed that she'd never taken the car to before.

Oliver turned around in his seat and slowly lifted his head to get a look.

His eyes must have glinted in the chasing car's headlights, because the second the light hit his face, a bullet flew straight over his head, flicking strands of his hair up as it went past.

'It's black,' Oliver said. He put a hand onto his chest and was not at all surprised to feel his heart thumping madly.

'How useful,' Lottie yelled from the front.

'Why don't you take a look?' Oliver shouted back, 'perhaps you could draw a picture too?'

'Quiet!' Anna said, taking her eyes off the road for a fraction of a second. 'And keep your heads down!' Lottie and Oliver stopped shouting.

'I think it's Holzmann!' Hugo shouted.

'Who?' Andrea shouted back.

'A Gestapo officer in our town. Doesn't like us very much,' Hugo said. There was a loud thud as a bullet went straight into the back of Andrea's seat. Something had stopped it from cleaving her in two.

'Whatever gives you that idea?' Andrea asked sarcastically.

'Be quiet!' Lottie yelled back.

'How long until the border?' Jens asked almost immediately.

'How on earth should I know?' Anna shouted, 'I haven't seen any signs.' The road seemed to be getting wider, but Anna still had to swerve to avoid another car.

'Isn't the border just the Rhine?' Oliver asked.

'I think we'll know if we drive through a river Oliver,' Anna said, her nerves beginning to fray.

'All I'm saying is that after we go past the Rhine we'll be safe, won't we?' Oliver asked.

'That's the plan,' Anna said, 'but with him, I don't know if he'll stop!'

Hugo was beginning to hope that the person shooting at them had run out of bullets; there hadn't been a gunshot for a while. Then the left wing mirror was blown off. Oliver risked another look at Holzmann's car, and he jumped when he saw how much closer it'd come. He couldn't be more than ten metres away.

'He's catching up,' Oliver shouted. Anna pushed the accelerator further into the carpet, but the car was already going faster than it was supposed to…there was no more in it.

'The road's sloping up,' Hugo said. Oliver looked ahead and clapped with excitement.

'That's a bridge!' he said. It was too close for Anna to slow down before they got to it, so he got ready for the impact of landing on the other side.

'Grab onto something!' Anna shouted as they hit the bridge. The car must have flown a good three metres into the air, and it hit the ground nose first.

A few seconds after, they heard Holzmann's car do something similar. Oliver didn't know what he'd expected, but Holzmann was chasing them as fervently as he had before.

'He's still there,' Oliver said.

'Really?' Anna shouted incredulously. 'I had no idea! I thought he was just going to stop at the bridge and go home!' Oliver didn't say anything after that.

Anna could see the lights of a town up ahead, and she began to plan.

They thundered into the town, making an absolute racket. Anna was willing the car to make as much noise as possible, and it happily obliged, spluttering and choking as she slowed down.

'Why are we slowing down?' Hugo shouted. He felt like a bit of an idiot when he realised how much the wind had gone down and how loud he sounded.

'I've got a plan,' Anna said. 'Quickly, everyone out of the car.' She'd come to a stop in the middle of the town.

The six of them got out as quickly as they could, no questions asked. Their legs were a little shaky after the drive, but they held firm.

Their entrance had attracted a few of the townsfolk, and Holzmann's entrance attracted even more. For a second, Anna was worried he would just run them down, but Holzmann slowed to a stop and hopped out of his car.

He pulled his gun from its holster and fired a shot into the sky. Anna actually smiled; it was as if he knew exactly what she wanted him to do.

'That was fun,' Holzmann said, the beginnings of a triumphant smile on the edges of his face, 'but your road ends here.'

'Here in Switzerland?' Anna asked. Holzmann looked slightly less confident.

'What does the country matter?' he said, 'you can either come with me or die where you stand.'

'Not in a neutral country,' Andrea said. She had planned to keep her mouth shut and let Anna talk, but she couldn't help herself.

'And what would you know about that?' Holzmann asked, as condescendingly as he could.

'I know that if you killed us here, the Swiss would declare war,' Andrea said. Holzmann laughed aloud.

'What could this paltry country do against the might of the German army?' he asked loftily. Andrea smirked. About a year ago, they had studied Switzerland at War School, and learnt why it was the last country on the list of places that would be invaded.

'It would stretch the German army too thin,' Andrea began, 'we're already fighting on two other fronts. A third would be impossible,' she paused. 'As well as that, this paltry country happens to have one of the best armies in the world, as well as an underground tunnel system. And if it came to it, the Swiss have rigged the mountain passes with explosives, and they are the only ways an army could move in and out of the country.' She felt extremely smug at the surprise on Holzmann's face, and the look she was getting from Anna only served to massage her ego.

'Are you still a German?' Holzmann demanded.

'Yes I am,' Andrea said.

'Then do what is right by the country that's brought you up like a mother would, and hand them over to me,' Holzmann told her.

He couldn't have known it, but to, some extent this struck a chord with Andrea. War School had been her home since her parents had died, and her brother was currently fighting for the country she was about to abandon.

But Andrea shook her head. 'No,' she said quietly. She stopped herself from thinking about how she could help Holzmann and steeled herself. 'I won't do that,' she said.

'Took you an awfully long time to decide,' Holzmann said.

'But she's decided,' Hugo said. She looked at him thankfully, and he nodded his head.

'Fine,' Holzmann shrugged as if it was of no consequence to him and he raised his gun. 'Who wants to die first?'

'Why not let the audience decide?' Hugo asked curtly, pointedly looking around.

Holzmann hadn't noticed people coming out of their houses to see what had disturbed their town, and there were easily a hundred people watching him point his gun. At first he thought he could ward them all off with a couple of warning shots, but he looked carefully at the assembled crowd and saw more than a few rifles.

Holzmann dropped his gun and walked up to the Safins and their friends. He walked until he stood a foot away from Hugo, and he looked him in the eyes. The hatred in his face was almost impossible to comprehend; Hugo hoped he never again met anyone that wanted to kill him as much as Holzmann did.

'I hate you,' he said softly. Hugo couldn't see any harm in baiting him a little, and he put a hand out for him to shake.

Holzmann roared and prepared to punch Hugo, but a bullet whistled over his head.

The man who fired it was, Hugo saw at once, a Swiss policeman. The policeman had a look on his face that told Holzmann that the miss hadn't been an accident. He waved the gun towards the car that Holzmann had come in, his message clear.

Holzmann took one last look at the Safins and their friends, before he turned and walked back towards his car. He started the engine violently, and very nearly hit a man on his way out.

When the black car faded from view, there was a collective sigh of relief and the townsfolk began to peter away.

The Swiss policeman walked up to them, smiling.

'Are you all OK?' he asked.

'I think we're a little shaken, but otherwise fine,' Anna said. 'Thank you all so much for what you did.' The man shook his head.

'It's really nothing,' he said. 'We just did what was right.'

'Thank you at any rate,' Anna said.

'Do you need somewhere to stay?' he asked.

'No, thanks, we're heading to my in-laws' house,' Anna said.

'Whereabouts is that?' the man asked.

'In Reinach,' Anna said. 'I'd like to get there before it's too late, so if you don't mind...' the man realised that he had been prying a little and he stepped back and smiled.

'No problem,' he said. 'You'll always be welcome here in Magden,' Anna shook the man's hand and led Hugo, Lottie and their friends back towards the car.

They got in and Anna fired up the engine.

'Mother?' Lottie asked as the car drove slowly out of the border town.

'Yes Lottie?' Anna replied.

'Are we really going to have to go to school?' Lottie asked. Anna sighed, and when they were free from Magden, she gave the accelerator a firm jab and sped away.

31

All's well

Hugo was, for the first time in three long years, completely carefree.

His room was a good size, and his bed was thicker and more comfortable than even his old one at War School. Or perhaps it was the lack of stress that made it feel that way. He was lying in this bed at the moment, recovering from Christmas two days before.

While he didn't celebrate Christmas, Hanukkah had come and gone during his stay at War School and so his mother had made the executive decision to celebrate Christmas as a replacement. The presents had mostly been clothes, bought for Andrea, Oliver and Jens, who hadn't expected to be living in Switzerland when they first packed.

He had met his father's parents for the first time as well, but they had treated him so lovingly in the past week that he began to wonder whether he hadn't known them his whole life. They seemed happy to just have people around the house, and it was a testament to the building's size that there were still spare rooms.

Hugo heard his door open, but he wasn't ready to wake up just yet, he'd stayed up awfully late the night before. It was probably his mother, coming to tell him to stop being lazy.

He felt a likeable, familiar, weight climb on to him. A few seconds passed before he heard a clap, only a few inches away from his ear.

'Wake up,' she said, smiling impishly.

'I'm awake, I'm awake,' Hugo said, rubbing his eyes and yawning, 'to what do I owe this pleasure?'

'I want to go for a swim,' Andrea asked.

'Can't we go later...?' Hugo said, sitting up.

'No, I want to go now,' Andrea said, pinning him to the bed. There was a knock at the door, and it opened before Hugo could reply.

Oliver took two steps into the room and a grin spread on his face when he saw the two of them.

The only thing keeping their situation from being completely compromising was the duvet between them.

Oliver coughed. 'Your grandmother wants to know if you want any breakfast or if you're just going to eat lunch later.'

'I'm all right,' Hugo said. 'So is Andrea, I think.'

'I can see that,' Oliver said, with a smile. He turned to leave but he remembered something and swivelled back. 'I almost forgot,' he said, 'you're all getting school uniforms this afternoon. So your mother's told me to tell you to be in the house and ready to leave by three.'

Anna had made good on her promise to enrol them all in a school, but due to his alleged genius and education at War School, Oliver had been allowed to enrol at university in the next academic year. This meant Oliver had nothing but free time for the next nine months, and he was extremely smug about it.

'Sure,' Hugo said.

'I'll leave you two alone,' Oliver said, closing the door as he walked out. Andrea hopped off the bed.

'I'll be waiting downstairs,' she said. She gave Hugo a quick kiss before leaving his room.

After he'd washed and got dressed, Hugo made his way down one of the house's several staircases. Slung over his shoulder was a drawstring bag that held his trunks.

Hugo could hear the sound of messy piano playing from the front lounge and followed it. He pushed the door open and found Jens and Lottie huddled on a single piano stool. There was another, older piano on the other side of the room, but the one they were playing was black and shiny. The second Hugo's grandparents had heard about Jens's prowess, they'd bought him a grand piano. They said it was a Christmas present, but Hugo suspected they would have bought it for him if it were July.

Jens said it was a Bösendorfer, and he had practically wet himself when it had come. Hugo didn't really know what the fuss was about; it sounded exactly the same as the other one.

Andrea was watching them play, and she got to her feet when she saw Hugo come in. Watching Lottie play had become a shared pastime for Hugo and Andrea. She didn't seem to have any talent as a pianist at all, and they enjoyed watching her struggle.

'We're going to the lake,' Andrea announced, one foot out of the door.

'See you,' Lottie said humourlessly.

Andrea had been in the front lounge for a good reason. There were only two ways in and out of the building, large as it was, and she had become lost on more than one occasion. The front lounge was only a few paces away from the front door.

It was a clear day outside, and they walked without haste.

'Hugo, I'd have talked to you an awful lot more at War School if I'd known how rich you were,' Andrea said.

'I'm not rich personally,' Hugo said. 'My dad's family is really old. I think we might even have a crest.'

Andrea laughed. 'You're definitely rich personally,' she said. 'You probably won't have to work a day in your life.'

'Then neither will you,' he said. Andrea went red, and her step slowed a little.

'No, Hugo, I always want to work. I need my life to have purpose.'

He smiled. 'So do I. I always want to work too.'

Neither of them said anything else until they arrived at the lake and changed. Hugo was about to jump in from the edge when Andrea called at him.

'Not from there!' she said, 'remember what Oliver did?' Oliver had come to the lake the day after they arrived and attempted to jump in from more or less where Hugo was now. To his surprise, the lake was only about two feet deep this close to the edge, and he had sprained his ankle.

Hugo nodded and slipped in, Andrea following close after him.

They waded out towards the middle of the lake, where the water was far deeper.

Hugo was not the world's best swimmer. He could tread water and his front crawl was passable, but he was slightly worried that Andrea would make him look an idiot.

She started to swim rings around him, not quickly but with a perfect technique. Hugo was convinced she was mocking him, and he flicked his wrist to send a spout of water at her face.

It would seem that Hugo was far better at pushing water than he was at swimming through it, because he hit her straight on the nose.

She turned straight away and splashed him back, using both hands.

There was a little back and forth before Hugo tried a particularly voracious push and Andrea caught his wrist.

Then they began to wrestle.

On land, Hugo would probably have beaten Andrea fairly quickly, but water was her element, so to speak.

At one point, Hugo had the ascendancy, and Andrea was struggling to break free of his grip.

Then she went limp. Her arms slacked, and Hugo released her in surprise. She sank slowly, and Hugo could only watch in horror as she faded from view.

He couldn't see her and he couldn't search for her, his eyes not used to being open underwater. He swam around, looking for bubbles or anything that would point him to her. There was nothing.

Then he felt a rush, as the water beside him was displaced upwards. Andrea popped up next to him as if there'd been an underwater diving board springing her upwards, her face red and breathing heavily.

The relief threatened to pull him under, but he was also a tad annoyed at her.

'Why on earth would you do that?' he asked her.

'I can't believe you were about to give up searching,' Andrea said with mock anger.

'I wasn't,' said Hugo indignantly. 'But how can you have held your breath for that long?'

'I just swam off down there and came up for air,' she said, pointing towards the water's edge.

She was very close to him. Less than a foot. He meant to take hold of her quickly, but the water slowed his arms down. The end result was the same though.

They held each other's gaze for a fair few seconds, and Hugo brought her in closer.

'HUGO! ANDREA!' it was Lottie. She was stood on the shore, waving her arms, 'YOU HAVE TO COME BACK RIGHT NOW! SOMETHING'S HAPPENED!'

'Later?' Andrea whispered the question into his mouth.

A shiver of anticipation and happiness surged through Hugo's body. He smiled at the woman he loved.

'Later,' he agreed.

'What's this news then?' Hugo asked. His hair was still wet, and he was stood in the kitchen with every other person in the house.

'Shhh,' Anna said. Oliver was trying to find the right station, and eventually he got it, tuning in halfway through a report.

'...has been declared missing. In other news, there have been several confirmed sightings of Joseph Stalin on the eastern front. Stalin, who was announced dead a week ago, was seen, in one instance, leading a line of tanks into battle. Soldiers who witnessed the spectacle said that bullets went straight though him, and he didn't seem to have a problem with the mud. Soldiers also noted that bullets that came close or appeared to hit would make Stalin stumble, but none of them stopped him.

After the tanks were captured, further inspection revealed a small, projector-like box to be the source of what is now known to be a projection of Joseph Stalin. This technology is clearly designed to project an illusion of Stalin's physical appearance, while keeping him safe from perils such as an assassin's bullet. He has since appeared on Soviet radio making statements and rallying his forces. He is reported to be alive and well.'

Oliver turned off the radio and looked at Jens.

'My God, I'm free of it!' Jens said. 'I don't need to have Stalin's death on my conscience for a moment longer!'

There was a cheer and Lottie made her way over to Jens.

"All that fuss for nothing!' she said. She put her arms around Jens and hugged him.

'The fuss wasn't all for nothing,' Jens replied, a smile stretching from ear to ear. 'I wouldn't be here with you otherwise.'

'No, maybe not,' Lottie said, 'we might not have ended up here, but there's no way I'd be anywhere without you.' She shrugged. 'So Stalin wasn't really killed at all.' Jens shook his head with a smile, but the second after the corners of his mouth stopped curving up, they flattened and he looked sombre again.

'What is it?' Lottie asked

'I was just thinking,' Jens murmured. 'What I said just now about not being here with you otherwise, maybe it wasn't true. After all, if I wasn't here I'd be at War School, but you...'

'Would probably be there too,' Lottie finished, she took his hand and squeezed it.

Jens gave a nod. 'Lottie, I've heard unspeakably ghastly terrible things about the Nazi concentration camps. The thought of you – and Hugo, and your mum, anywhere near those places makes me feel sick.'

'Yes, and it should make you feel sick,' Lottie said. 'But please stop thinking about it Jens. The Nazis can't touch us in Switzerland.'

Jens looked as if the safety of their current situation had just dawned on him. A smile of childish joy spread across his face and he picked her up by the waist and spun her around. Lottie laughed at Jens's manner and how quickly it could change – a few seconds before he had been positively miserable.

'What was that for?' she asked with a smile after Jens had put her down.

'I'm so happy!' Jens said in a voice much younger than his frame.

'You've been happy before,' Lottie said, reining in her smirk.

'Not like this I haven't,' Jens said. 'I've never felt like this before and I can't think how to describe it to you.'

He thought for a few more seconds before he realised what he wanted to say couldn't possibly be put into words. He took hold of Lottie's face and kissed her, articulating his thoughts and feelings in one swift movement.

'Oh, darling,' Lottie said softly. Jens laughed and kissed her again.

Outside the kitchen, Oliver was stood alone, thinking. It was symbolic of the journey that they had taken that the nephew of Joseph Goebbels had fallen for a Jewish girl, and it suggested a much brighter future than the one they had left behind in Germany. He began to smile – this was the beginning of their lives.

PART FOUR:

Epilogue

The subsequent lives of the people you've been reading about...

LOTTIE SAFIN AND JENS GOEBBELS

Jens's surname was a major handicap in Switzerland, and he struggled to integrate with the other children at his new school. He spent his days avoiding his classmates, and his evenings shut away in his room, keeping himself to himself. Lottie was the only person who could bring a smile out of him, and apart from school, the piano was the only thing that brought him out of his room.

The music teachers at his school had been asking Jens to play with the orchestra since they had first heard him play, and when he eventually did, he was so brilliant that he found himself with a perfect opportunity for a fresh start.

He was offered a scholarship to study at the Conservatoire de Music de Genève, the oldest music school in the country. The prospect of being around a new crowd of people who knew nothing of him or his family was irresistible, and he gladly accepted the place. Before he left for Geneva, Jens had his surname legally changed to Friedlander, his mother's maiden name, so severing the last ties to his Nazi past.

Lottie was devastated when Jens left for music school. She understood why he had to go, and was happy for him, but with Jens two hundred kilometres away in Geneva, she began to feel acutely alone. She saw Jens once a month whilst he was away, and they wrote to each other as often as the post allowed, but it was never enough for either of them. Her art began to take up more of her time in the months after Jens left, and she would travel into town at weekends to sell her paintings.

Two years later, when Jens was due to finish at music school, an American art-dealer came across Lottie and the paintings that adorned her small stall. He was enthralled by her ability, especially when it came to painting buildings, and he suggested that she try architecture as a way to better utilise her gift. In his awe, the art dealer offered to recommend Lottie to the Dean at the University of California, Berkeley.

This raised a problem for Lottie – Jens had done so well at the conservatoire that he seemed likely to be joining the prestigious Tonhalle Orchestra in Zurich, one of the dozens that had invited him to play.

Because Lottie was going to be in California, Jens decided instead to accept an offer he had received from the much smaller San Francisco Symphony Orchestra. Lottie was delighted, and the two of them set off for California in 1950.

After studying, Lottie began remaking as much of the world as she was commissioned to; her unique designs and understanding of shape meant that she was often asked to design houses for the rich and famous living in Palo Alto.

Her first architectural credit, however, was far from the exotic mansions that she would spend the next twenty years designing: It was the small synagogue in which she and Jens were married.

Lottie and Jens decided not to have children but chose instead to devote themselves to their professions.

Jens was the San Francisco Symphony's pianist for ten years, before moving into a role as a conductor, and composing pieces of his own. Music began to take up more and more of his life as time went on, and where once there was joy, there was stress and pressure. He had taken on far too much, and was unwilling to accept help.

A heart attack in 1975 was a warning sign. Despite all Lottie's support and help, Jens continued to work too hard and unfortunately, Jens died of a second heart attack in 1976, aged only fifty-one.

Jens's untimely death never completely left Lottie, and she refused to remarry, wearing her wedding ring on her middle finger in memory of him. Lottie was on the first flight back to Switzerland after the funeral – the heat of the Californian sun had become stifling, and she longed for the company of family.

Lottie still lives in Reinach with Hugo and Andrea.

OLIVER MULLER

In 1942, at the age of sixteen, Oliver began a physics degree at ETH Zurich – the best university in Switzerland. He finished top of his year, and carried on in Zurich until he had earned a PhD in the cutting-edge field nuclear physics.

Oliver was invited to the US to work for the Atomic Energy Commission (AEC), an organisation developing nuclear weapons after the war. He was posted in and around the Pacific Islands, the region favoured by the Americans for nuclear tests.

Two decades working in the Pacific Islands brought him close to the islanders and their culture, and he struck up an unlikely but blissfully happy relationship with a young schoolteacher called Hara. She had been displaced by the tests on the Bikini Atoll, and Oliver and Hara were married in 1955, on the island of Hawaii.

In 1968, at the age of forty-four, Oliver received an invitation to lecture at University College, Oxford in England. After twenty years spent designing weapons with the AEC, Oliver felt the need for a change and presented the idea to his wife. Hara wasn't keen to trade the warmth of the Pacific for the tepid clouds of England, but the opportunity to settle down proved too tempting.

The peace of the city was a stark contrast to the explosions of his time with the AEC, and Oliver and Hara fell in love with the place. Hara took up teaching at the Oxford Girls School, and Oliver lectured until 1990, when he and his wife retired.

Oliver and Hara still live in Oxford today, and whilst they are a little too old to be constantly flying back to Reinach to see Oliver's friends, technology means that they can talk to Hugo, Lottie, and Andrea to their heart's content. They are all now friends on Facebook.

ANDREA DUCASSE AND HUGO SAFIN

Andrea and Hugo had an idyllic two years in Switzerland after their time at War School. Despite being given rooms at opposite ends of the Safin house, they were never out of each other's company for too long.

Once they had finished school, however, a separation began to seem inevitable – Andrea had her heart set on training to be an army officer in England, at the Royal Military Academy, Sandhurst. She'd faced a tremendous battle to get them to even consider her application, being as she was, a young woman, and she felt like arriving with her boyfriend would give the wrong impression.

1946, a year in which Hugo only saw Andrea half a dozen times, was incredibly difficult for him – he loved her very much, and missed her a great deal. He took to writing to pass the time, trying his hand at a story or two before realising that his talent lay in journalism. He submitted several articles to the local paper, who enjoyed his hopeful takes on the post-war world so much that they brought him on as a columnist.

Andrea returned from Sandhurst in 1947 to find a boyfriend politicised by his writing. She had long been passionate about politics, and the nights they spent together became all the more intimate, as their sweet nothings were joined by debate and discussion.

When Hugo proposed to Andrea in late 1950, the only question asked was why it had taken him so long – it had been clear for years that they were made for each other. They were married in a small, intimate ceremony in front of the Safin house, and in place of a honeymoon, the couple travelled to South Korea; Andrea as an army officer, and Hugo as a journalist. This was the pattern for the next five years: they jetted around the world as a couple, and Hugo wrote wonderful articles about his wife's adventures.

They went on in chaotic harmony until 1956, when their lives of travel and adventure were disturbed by Andrea's pregnancy, and the eventual birth of their daughter, Emily. She changed things, as children tend to – where once Hugo and

Andrea had craved excitement, they now had a tremendous desire for safety and a permanent home. Andrea especially knew exactly what it was to grow up without parents, and she would not let the same happen to her daughter.

They returned to the house in Reinach with Emily as soon as it was possible, and settled into family life. Hugo continued to write, but Andrea took on a role consulting the Swiss Army, staying well out of any active conflict.

Emily grew up in a serenity and comfort that her parents could only have dreamed of, a fact they were keen to remind her of as she got older. The result was the inheritance of her parents' desire for adventure, and Emily followed her mother into a military career.

Hugo and Andrea can still be found in the house at Reinach, keeping a watchful eye on Lottie.

THE END

Acknowledgements

Any achievement, regardless of how big or small, is a result of work and effort from those ranging far beyond the person credited. This is especially the case with this endeavour, as without James Essinger, you would not be holding this book in your hands.

The first, c70,000-word draft of this book was written and 'finished' when I was thirteen, and James was the only literary agent willing to even consider taking on a client who had barely started secondary school. In the five years since then, his guidance and skill as an editor has been invaluable, and his knowledge of literature as an industry has been inexhaustible.

The human aspect of James's help has perhaps exceeded the rest of his contributions not just to this book, but the last five years of my life as a whole. Rugby and school commitments have meant that I have very regularly gone months without talking to James, or working on this novel, and every time I contact him, he has been exceptionally patient and helpful.

I am also extremely grateful to Annelisa Christensen for her very hard work on *War School*, her deep insights into both plot and character, and the encouragement she gave me with the story.

All credit for the striking cover of the book must go to Charlotte Mouncey, I'm not sure how she did it, but she captured the feeling of *War School* perfectly!

A tremendous amount of thanks is bestowed upon my parents by default, being as I am, their son; but the necessity of this acknowledgement should take nothing away from its magnitude. Everything my parents do is for the benefit of their children, and it has been eighteen years but I am still often amazed by the lengths that they go to for my brothers and me. It is not by accident that I grew up with a love of books – the environment cultivated by my mother and father made it an inevitability.

Having only left school a few months ago, it would be wrong not to thank every teacher unlucky enough to have taught me. A special mention must go to my English, Politics, and History teachers – I was only able to improve as a writer as a result of the essays and practice that your lessons gave me.

Friends give life colour and depth, and I thank anyone who has ever considered me a friend for the time that I have spent in your company. I have been lucky to rub shoulders with some absolutely spectacular people, and you can all feel free to claim to have been the inspiration for whoever you like.

All in all, the point is made above. Whilst I put a tremendous amount of work into this book, and proudly claim it as my own, I was only able to put it together because of the people around me.

I thank you all, and I thank you the reader for coming this far.

I hope this isn't the last thing I'll write!

Julian Manieson

*As an aside, by 'La Follia' (Chapter 10), I am referring to Vivaldi's Sonata No.12, Op. 1, Rv. 63, as performed by Il-Gardino Armonico.